REMEMBER ME

REMEMBER ME

YOLA DUNNE

LOVING MOTHER
EARTH PRESS

Loving Mother Earth Press

Book Layout and Cover Design: Gessert Books

Loving Mother Earth Press
181 Old Chelsea Road
Chelsea, Québec, J9B 1J3
Visit our website at www.lovingmotherearth.com

ISBN 978-0-9959797-1-0 (print)
ISBN 978-0-9959797-0-3 (ebook)

Printed in the United States of America
First Edition

For Oscar

—§—

CHAPTER ONE

My name is Carmen Agnes Sirota. I was born in Winnipeg, Canada. I was graced with an experience that awakened my courage and introduced me to the true meaning and purpose of my Life. But before I share this life transforming story, please allow me to tell you more about myself.

The name Carmen was given to me by my mother. She had a strange obsession with Bizet's famous work. For their honeymoon, my father took her all the way to the Metropolitan in New York City to see the famous opera. Father recounted that mother wept the whole way through and decreed she would name her first girl Carmen. What made mother's obsession with Carmen a little odd was that she was of First Nations ancestry. Not that there is anything unusual about being native and enjoying various forms of art, but mother took her love for "all things non-native" to the extreme. She died her black hair blonde, had countless European history books, and made a point of rejecting anything to do with her culture. She taught herself French, German and Spanish. We lived in a small farming community outside of Winnipeg, but mother looked and behaved as though she belonged on the high streets of Paris. My grandmother Agnes, whom I was also named after, would often joke with me: "Your mother is a true rebel warrior," she would say with heart. "One day she will find her way back to her roots, and you will help her." She paused and looked deeply into my eyes. "Remember child," she squeezed my hand. "You have much of your mother in you. One day you may face similar challenges, but you will have the courage to overcome them." I didn't quite understand what she meant, yet I could feel her profound love for both of us. Grandmother never reprimanded mother for her choices. She would let her be, and instead she would pour all her love into me and into her own life.

Father was a simple man. His grandfather had immigrated to Canada from the Ukraine hoping to start a better life. He was a young boy who had lost both of his parents and had no family. When the officer asked him his name for immigration, he responded 'sirota' which meant "orphan" in Russian; and that's how he received his Canadian name. My father was a role model for stamina and gentleness. These are qualities that he inherited from his ancestors who had worked so hard to make a life for themselves. He was a humble man and loved my mother deeply. Although he was not rich, he would lavish her with delicacies that one would only find in the big cities. She loved these and, as far as I could tell, also loved him very much. The life on the farm did not suit her well. Father would spend most of his working days out of the house, leaving her to her musings and imaginations. In my mother's case too much time alone did not benefit her. She became more extreme, spending days locked up in her room engulfed in reading books. She would also spend hours making clothes for herself. As time went on, she neglected me more and more, and father would drive me to see grandmother on the reservation a ways away. I didn't mind. I adored spending time with her.

Grandmother was a wise woman. Many considered her a medicine woman, but she would always deny it. "I am no medicine woman," she huffed. "I am merely a woman filled with life and wonder." And that she was. Her tribe came originally from the Upper Great Lakes. She had met her husband at a pow wow which brought her to Manitoba. She would bake bannock on an open flame and was renowned as a master canoe maker. She felt canoe building was an endangered art and did everything she could to pass on her knowledge. She would spend hours with me showing me this and that, always a story and a song on her lips, and a smile from her soul. I loved her very much and cherished each moment with her.

Then one day as grandmother and I were returning from the store, a fight broke out at a neighbour's home. Grandmother approached the drunk men, attempting to get a closer look at what was happening. One of the men got startled by her approach, thinking it was someone who was going to fight him. He turned around forcefully and jabbed a knife in her belly. When he saw who it was he was horrified and backed up instantly, but it was too late. The knife had gone too deep. Grandmother fell awkwardly backward and sat on the grass, clutching the knife. I ran towards her screaming. One of the men shouted for someone to call an ambulance, but we all knew that was futile. The reserve was an hour away from any urgent medical care. They would not reach us in time. I cried as I held her hand. The wound was painful and had made irreversible damage, and she knew it. She was fading quickly. "It's alright child," she said under a painful breath. "We all have our time to go. And this is mine. I am going home to Great Spirit now, and I go with peace. I have lived a good life." I looked at her in dismay, balling. She winced from the pain and continued, "Carmen, promise me you will forgive this man. Forgive him." I cried even harder. How could that even be possible, I thought? Grandmother collapsed on the ground. I took my jacket and laid it under her head. She kept her eyes closed for a moment, and when she opened them again, she was imbued with a serene presence. Time stood still. We looked at one another in silence until she uttered, "I love you Carmen. I will always love you." Then she was gone.

I was 10 years old when grandmother died, and nothing was the same again. Although my mother never outwardly showed affection or care towards grandmother, the news of her death devastated her. It was the catalyst that brought her to the bottle and pushed her to the limits of her sanity. She became so violent towards my father, that he would rarely come home. He tried everything to help her, but it only made mother reject him more. His broken heart was palpable. She never laid a hand on me, but sometimes I wished she did, so I could feel that I was alive. Instead, she completely ignored me. One day she decided that she had had enough of the farm and her life, packed her belongings, and moved to the city. I went with her.

The years in Winnipeg were rocky at best. Most of the time they were spent cleaning up after mother and trying to go to school. Mother found a cheap apartment and started to waitress down the street at a local diner. Not at all the bourgeois life she always imagined for herself. The job was enough to pay the rent and for her booze. Occasionally she would fill the fridge with food, but it was up to me to ration it and fend for myself. In the beginning father would come by to buy me clothes and make sure I had everything for school. It was always so nice to see him, and I wondered why I did not remain on the farm with him. He always said I was welcomed there, but I told him that I needed to stay with mother. Without me she would have nobody. So I stayed by her side. Most times she continued to ignore me, and I blamed the behaviour on the alcohol. There were moments when she was sober, that I felt I had a mother again. She would embrace me and cry, and say how sorry she was for the life she had given me. We would then go to the movies and have a good time, and these were the times when I felt I was normal. But they were few and far between. Her illness became so bad that I had to wake her up at 4pm for her shift, and it took great effort to get her out the door.

The scent of alcohol oozed out of her pores. How she managed to keep working during these times is beyond my comprehension. She could not tolerate the sight of my father anymore, so he stopped coming over. He would secretly buy me food credits at a grocery store nearby, and we would meet for lunch when I was at school. We never spoke about mother. Then one fall day, we received the news from an old neighbour that father had had an accident on the farm. He was at a local hospital in critical condition. Mother refused to go see him, and I had no means to go. My father died a couple of days after the accident. And he took a part of me with him.

The next few years were a blur. To be frank I have worked hard to shut them out of my mind, and I don't want to recall them here. Suffice it to say that mother got worse, and our apartment became the stomping ground for many of the local addicts and drunks. It made living at home almost impossible. I was 17 when I left Winnipeg. I needed a fresh start. It was a matter of life or death. I knew that if I did not take my life into my own hands, I would end up living in the streets permanently. I instinctively knew the streets would turn me into a ghost or kill me. I had too much of my mother's blood in me. So I scraped together enough money for a bus ticket and made my way to Calgary. I never said goodbye to mother, and I never looked back.

I went directly to the welfare office when I arrived in Calgary and explained my situation. They helped me right away. There was a room in a halfway house available, and they gave me food stamps to get by. Within two weeks, I had found work at McDonald's; and within a month, I had my own place. It wasn't fancy, but it was clean and safe. I didn't like my job very much but was grateful to have it. I managed to tune out my past the best I could. I did this to survive. Unfortunately, it also meant that I pushed away all the good memories along with the bad. The only things I was clutching to were my survival instincts and my determination never to follow in my mother's footsteps. It appears that fear is often a good motivator.

A year later, a specialty coffee shop opened up in the neighbourhood. They served organic coffee and other fair trade items. I loved the place as soon as I saw it. It gave me a warm, homey feeling, and I instantly knew I wanted to work there. I took a deep breath, took a chance and walked in. And I walked out with a new job. The three years I worked at the coffee shop were filled with good memories. Times were simple and provided a much needed respite from my previously tumultuous life. The routine was good for me. Month by month I felt like I developed my own personality, and I liked who I was becoming. I often thought of mother. Every once in a while, I would think of contacting her, but something deep inside me would stop me in my tracks. So I kept to myself and focused on my work and my life.

CHAPTER TWO

I met Richard at the coffee shop. He would come in at least once a day to have a black coffee. There was a private nook looking onto the street, and he would often meet his clients there. He was always very kind to me and took interest in who I was. I never told him much about my life, and he never pried. I admired his demeanor and how he always had something good and uplifting to say. No wonder he was one of the most successful Realtors in the country. Over a couple of years, I got to know him well, and he eventually made me an offer to work for him as his administrative assistant. I was 21.

The Real Estate business was a natural fit for me. I worked really hard, going above and beyond what was asked of me. Richard was patient with me and taught me everything I needed to know. I never told him I hadn't completed high school, but somehow I sensed he knew already. I started with simple tasks like filing documents and cleaning the office until I became proficient enough to prepare legal documents and sales pitches. Soon Richard discovered that I had an affinity for writing descriptions of properties. I became so good at it that he had me come to the client's homes to take photos and notes, and even interview the seller, so I could write more about the houses. The properties I detailed sold quickly. I also began to give some advice on decor and how to make a few changes to the homes, so they would be more attractive to buyers.

I also had a knack for really getting to know our clients who were buyers. Because I had photographic memory, I would rarely miss any details of any listing from other realtors. I knew the specs of the properties inside out. After in-depth interviews with our clients, I had a very good sense of what type of home they were looking for and what they could afford. Richard kept encouraging me along the way, sending me to courses, and giving me more and more responsibilities.

Ours was an affectionate relationship, a father-daughter relationship. I had missed my father dearly, especially because of his premature death. Richard filled that gap for me. He was a kind, fair, and hard working man. He had grown up on a farm, and in those days, much was expected from a young man. He would spend many days tending the family farm, and on the side he would renovate old houses. At first he did it to help the old folk. He had the gift of the gab, and people immediately trusted and loved him. One day a widowed neighbour asked if he could help her renovate her house in exchange for a small property adjacent to hers. Over a few months, he managed to work on the farm and renovate her home, which sold for a good price in the spring. He then did the same with the small home given to him - this is how the real estate business came to him.

I continued to work hard, and within three years I became a realtor. After another couple of years, Richard made me a partner in the firm. I was satisfied with my accomplishments. I believed one could achieve anything they set their mind to if they were determined, worked hard, and wanted it strongly. I naïvely thought my life stood on a solid foundation. I also felt a lot of pride that I had made something out of myself and avoided what could have been a life of addiction and suffering. I depended upon my career driven personality to push me forward and developed a flourishing business in real estate. I lived in a trendy part of the city, owned a few revenue properties, and was physically fit. My regular routine consisted of buying a latté or two every day and making sure that I made it to yoga at least four times a week. I took good care of my health and particular care in keeping up my professional appearance. I had a select group of friends, and we got together often to experience the latest food and wine trends and for trivial chitchat. Once in a while, I would volunteer at the local food bank to serve a meal to the homeless until that became impractical. I discovered that gathering donations would be more effective, so every year my firm would gather the largest donation of food in the city and present it to the food bank. I thought this was a perfect marketing tool for my real estate business, contributing to those who had no homes. This made me feel like I was giving back to the community and less guilty for my success. Still, a part of me could not understand how people could remain in a homeless situation. Because I had gotten myself out of homelessness, I secretly thought that others also had the duty and responsibility to get themselves back on their feet. A part of me did not accept those who were too weak to change their lives. I believed I was a living example of success. So why weren't the homeless and destitute helping themselves more? But I kept these thoughts to myself. I believed what I was doing was meaningful and felt nothing could bring me down. Until the unthinkable happened. And this is where my story really begins. Let me introduce you to Larry.

Richard had two children, Sophia and Larry. Sophia was gifted with a keen intellect and was off to medical school at the University of British Columbia. She was the first one in both her father's and mother's families to go University, let alone medical school. Everyone was very proud of her. Larry was quite the opposite of his older sister. He never knew what he wanted out of life and repeatedly got in trouble with the law. He loved to gamble and pick fights in bars, which got him arrested on more than one occasion. He had a lust for fast cars, beautiful women, and was known to be quite the charmer. He desired to be part of his father's business, yet his father wanted him to have more life experience and show that he could be responsible. To satisfy his father, Larry finally agreed to go to business school. His newfound knowledge increased his lust for money and beautiful things. After he graduated, he became a luxury car salesman and was very successful at it. He went ahead and got his realtor licence, and after repeatedly asking his father to be part of the family business, Richard finally gave him a few properties to sell.

Larry surprised everyone by how well he did with the sales. He had the gift of the gab like his father, and people believed what he told them. He worked hard and quit his job as a car salesman. Many of his previous customers came to him for advice about buying and selling commercial properties and luxury homes. What he accomplished in a short time was astonishing. Larry had opened up a new income stream for the business through commercial real estate, and the business grew exponentially. His father was impressed and thought that perhaps he had been too old school in his methods and expectations for his son. Clearly Larry had a knack for business, and after a year of probation, he offered him full partnership in the firm. No one could blame him. Larry was his son after all, and it was clear that he added something significant to the business.

I, however, was suspicious of Larry. Something just didn't sit right with me. I wondered if I was jealous, which could have been the case. In the beginning I had Richard all to myself, and now I shared his attention with his son. Also, Larry was never welcoming of me. Most times I felt like an imposter, and I couldn't explain why. Larry hated his older sister, who was the jewel of the family, and I guessed I must have reminded him of her. It was clear he wasn't keen on me having such a close relationship with his father. He would often take me aside and tell me that no matter what I did, I would never be as good as he was, and to remember that he had priority over me because he was Richard's son. I never spoke about this with his father. I didn't see the point in doing so. I decided to trust the relationship Richard and I had built together and the business partnership. Regardless of the hiccups, Larry and I managed to get along fine. There was so much work to do, and we each had our divisions to take care of. Together, we became the top grossing real estate firm in the country.

It wasn't long after we reached the top of our field that Richard got diagnosed with an aggressive form of lung cancer. By the time it was discovered, the cancer had already spread to his lymphatic system. The news was devastating. Sophia was now doing her residency in pediatrics and was very busy but came to be with her father whenever she could. It was a tough time for everyone. He passed away within three months of the initial diagnosis, leaving Larry as the majority shareholder in the company.

It was difficult to digest Richard was gone. He had been my mentor and beloved friend. I learned to tolerate Larry mostly to please Richard. Now that he was gone, the weight of responsibility became heavier to bear. But to prove myself strong and capable, I doubled my efforts and put my nose to the grindstone. I was determined to keep the business going as if nothing had happened. I became so focused that I did not see what was going on right before my eyes.

Larry did well when he first joined the firm, keeping his gambling penchant to sports and poker. His betting became well known in the office, but no one thought more of it. His father's presence kept him in check, but the taste for power never left him. What his father so diligently built was not enough for him. In fact he would often laugh at his father's old and ethical ways. One day he announced he wanted to grow the company and open a satellite office in Vancouver, which he would run. That worked perfectly for me. I could continue running the office in Calgary and get him out of my hair. It seemed like a perfect plan.

In the beginning, I was impressed by the profits. Larry bought many properties in a short period of time, turning them over rapidly and making a good return in the process. He bought an old building downtown, renovated it, and made it into a trendy sushi bar. What I didn't know is that the bar was a cover for prostitution, organized crime, money laundering, cocaine trafficking, and major real estate fraud. I was so busy running the company in Calgary, I did not know what was going on until the police came to my door with a warrant to search the company and my personal home. I had no idea. I was completely bewildered. And because I was the only other shareholder, I was liable for my business partner's shenanigans. I felt like a complete idiot for not trusting my intuition and the signs along the way. I got too greedy, overlooking the obvious clues that would normally have someone's hair stand up at the back of their necks.

I simply couldn't believe it. Could Larry really be doing this to me? All these years I had put my complete trust in my business partners. I worked so hard to make my way up the ladder of success, and right beside me my business partner was lying and cheating, and I had absolutely no idea about it. Overnight, the world I knew so well crumbled. There are no words to describe how this betrayal affected me. How was this happening? I couldn't help but think that if Richard was still alive, none of this would have happened. I wanted to retreat into a cave and never come out again. I was sulking. How could someone's life be turned around that quickly? All those years of meticulous work, the long hours, the sacrifices; all for nothing. I was so angry, I was paralyzed. The only thing I could do was to claim defeat. I had lost everything. But my worst fear was to lose face, and this too happened. The company was closed down overnight. There was nothing I could have done to salvage it, even if I had caught on to Larry's activities earlier. Richard had willed the majority of the shares to his son, trusting that he would treat me fairly. It had been his dream to have a family business after all. Although my portion of the shares was significant and worth a large sum of money when Richard passed away, it was worthless now. So much debt had accumulated and was owed that the entire company needed to go into bankruptcy. I took refuge in yoga.

CHAPTER THREE

"Come on Carmen, cheer up!" Joni cajoled as she picked up her yoga mat. "This was a great class. And you did so well with the downward dog. Best I've seen you do so far!"

I was barely conscious of being in the class. My mind was hijacked with thoughts of Larry. "If Larry was in downward dog right now, I'd stuff…," I mumbled under my breath.

"What's that?" Joni asked innocently. "Nothing," I replied, tucking my mat under my arm.

Joni was a pearl. There was nothing not to like about her. She had one of those buoyant personalities that would light up a room wherever she went. She was a nurse and now taught at the Faculty of Nursing at the University of Calgary. We met at Shiva's Garden, the local trendy yoga studio, and hit it off instantly. From that day forward we attended most yoga classes together.

"I know you're in a bad situation, Carm," Joni offered in a more sober tone, clearly noticing my distress and lack of attention. "But you know all things happen for a reason. Maybe the real estate business has had enough of you. Maybe it's time for a change. Maybe one day you will see this as one of the most important periods of your life." She looked at me with an encouraging smile, hoping her words would cheer me up or at least change my attitude. All I wanted to do was hit her on the head with my yoga mat. There were times when optimism simply didn't taste right. Clearly I was not ready for an attitude adjustment. I changed the subject quickly, "Let's go for a smoothie." Like a Jack Russell terrier wanting to play ball, Joni perked up and could not resist the suggestion. She loved her smoothies. She did not try to cheer me up again that night. I was relieved.

Joni was unusually quiet and reserved when we met for our next yoga class. She asked if we could go for sushi after class because there was something she wanted to talk to me about. She looked at me in such an intense way that I was instantly alarmed.

"Are you okay? Is there something wrong?" I asked, feeling guilty for taking up so much air time in our friendship lately because of my predicament.

"Oh, I'm good, Carm. Don't worry about me. We can talk about it later."

That was a typical Joni response. Still, I was intrigued and curious. So much so that I was actually able to tune out thoughts of Larry and focus on doing yoga. It had been a while since I had had a good class. It was refreshing to stop thinking about myself for a change.

We didn't talk much as we made our way to the restaurant. Once we had ordered our meals and were sipping miso soup, Joni finally broke the awkward silence. I held my breath in anticipation of what she was about to say.

"You know, Carm, Peru has been on my bucket list for some time now," she looked at me as if she was confessing to a priest. I didn't know how to react, so I let her continue. "So I went ahead and booked a tour."

I finally let out a deep breath, not realizing I had been bracing myself for bad news. My relief was instantaneous. But before I could comment, she continued, "The thing is, you are coming with me."

She placed a couple of tickets on the table. I nearly choked on my soup. Joni just sat there looking guilty and observing my response. Was she serious? I put my soup down and took a closer look at the tickets. They were vouchers for a Sacred Mysteries Tour of Peru. One of the vouchers had my name on it. I couldn't believe it. Then my eyes zeroed in on the date.

"Joni! This tour starts in 2 weeks!"

"I know, Carm." Now she looked sheepish. "I took a chance, a big chance. But I knew you had all your immunizations from our trip to Bali last year." We had gone to a yoga retreat there last Christmas. "And because your life is in shambles, I thought that perhaps it would be good for you to get away from it all."

I was too stunned to respond. I looked at Joni, then the tickets, then back at Joni. She looked so sincere I couldn't help but give in. I relaxed. Her love was oozing out of her, and I knew her actions were coming out of sincere love for me. "But Joni, I can't accept this from you - it's too great a gift."

Joni perked up, "So you're saying it's a yes?"

Like I mentioned before, her enthusiasm was contagious. "Oh, alright. Why not!" Joni squealed with delight and nearly knocked the California rolls off the table.

She was right. It had been two months since my office had been shut down, and I had been miserable. At least the police had determined I had no involvement in Larry's criminal activities. It meant I was off the hook for being under criminal investigation. Yet I could not practice real estate until the affair settled, which could take months, even years. I had no choice in the matter; I had to wait it out. Three weeks in a foreign country could be a great way to escape my world. To be honest, I had no idea what else to do and how to make decisions about my life. I felt stuck and devoid of vitality. A part of me had died with the betrayal.

I don't remember much about the preparations. Luckily, Joni was the Queen of Organization and Googled every part of the tour beforehand. Joni gave me lists of items to bring, and all I needed to do was pack what was on her lists. Truth be told, I was grateful she took control of the preparations and made things simple for me. I did not realize how exhausted I was until I had to think. It was as if my brain got jumbled up, and I could not function like I used to.

Joni and I met for yoga and coffee a few times before our departure. She kept rambling off names I didn't recognize and talking about the Sacred Valley, Machu Picchu, and the chance to meet a real live shaman in the rainforest. Her 'joie de vivre' and excitement were refreshing. They provided me with the fuel I needed to keep going, even though it was mostly on fumes. She gave me a reason to have faith in humanity. If everyone had a Joni near them, the world would certainly be too amused to create strife and war.

I managed to get all my things packed an hour before I was scheduled to be picked up to go to the airport. I sat exhausted on my bed, wanting to curl up and forget about everything. I must have drifted off to sleep because the sound of the doorbell jolted me out of my slumber. It was Joni, just on time. She helped me lug my backpack to the taxi. Travelling with a backpack was completely new to me. I usually travelled with business attire and rolling suitcases. Backpacks were for hippies and world travellers, in my opinion. But Joni convinced me it would be easier to carry around while we traveled, so I went with it.

It was a cold November night and a blizzard was brewing. I hurriedly got into the taxi and slammed the door shut. If nothing of worth came out of this trip, at least I would get a break from this ungodly climate.

Unsurprisingly, we arrived at the airport hours before our departure time. Joni insisted this was the best way to proceed. To her credit, the airport was abnormally busy because of American Thanksgiving, combined with some flight delays prompted by the freak snow storm. Still, we were some of the first to check in for our flight. Joni graciously offered me the window seat. It was a nice gesture as she remembered that one of the few things I loved about traveling was to look out the tiny window onto the ever-changing landscape. It made me think. It was one of life's small pleasures for me.

While Joni was making final arrangements and perusing our travel documents like a detective, I made a beeline to Starbucks. I had already had a couple of lattes that day, but I figured this would be my last opportunity for decent coffee for some time. I ordered the largest size available. The display of baked goods was also tempting, and for once I decided to indulge myself and bought a scone. I stuffed it in my bag and walked back to find Joni.

She had already scouted a few other tour participants and was chatting with them as if she'd known them since childhood. I overheard one of them asking her if she was the organizer. She laughed with a high-pitched voice saying bashfully, "Oh, no! I'm only a participant." I wondered if it was the clipboard and stack of travel documents she carried that made them ask. She noticed me and grabbed my arm. I held on to my coffee for dear life.

"This is my friend Carmen! She's gone through a lot in the last little while, if you know what I mean." She winked at the middle-aged couple dressed in nearly identical travel gear. "We thought that a spiritual quest would do her some good." She beamed and showed me off like a prized poodle. A battered prized poodle that is.

Great. So much for anonymity. And in one appalling instant, I realized I had completely forgotten that we were on this trip as part of a tour. We would be meeting some of the participants at the Calgary airport and then joining the others in Lima. Because of all the upheaval, it had never dawned on me that I would be spending time with a group of strangers. I felt terribly ill as a wave of dread came over me. I clutched my coffee more feverishly.

The couple nodded and smiled politely. I wasn't sure if it was from sympathy or because they too had just realized they were stuck with me. Oh, dear. What had I gotten myself into? For a brief instant, I debated making a run for it. I could leave the airport and renege on the whole crazy thing. But frankly, I was too exhausted to care. Besides, I'd probably spill my coffee. So I smiled politely back, nodding in a "yep, that's poor me" kind of way. The couple looked back at Joni in unison. I was off the hook, thank goodness. I took advantage of the moment to slip away from the conversation and found a bench nearby. For what seemed like a blurry few minutes I waited patiently as Joni explained a few more details of the tour. How she had gathered all that information was beyond me.

"They're a nice couple!" Joni exclaimed as she joined me. I had gotten lost in my thoughts while people watching. I came back to reality. "Yes, they were charming," I replied. "I especially liked their outfits." Joni was oblivious to my sarcasm. When did I get so bitter? Oh, yes: Larry.

"Look! A spa!" Joni exclaimed. "Don't you love modern day travel? I remember the days when people smoked in airplanes and restaurants. You see, Carmen, the world is becoming a better place." Nothing could shake her optimism. I wondered if they sold some of that at Starbucks. I'd add a shot of it to my latté. "Come on. Let me treat you to a massage. It will be symbolic of a new beginning. You can leave all that tension behind, and you'll be nice and relaxed for the flight."

I didn't think a massage was a good idea. The thought of it gave me the creeps. I've never been at ease with a stranger touching me. My body was private territory, and I liked it that way. I gently broke the news to Joni. After some insisting on my part and bartering, we settled on a pedicure. Joni ordered an oxygen boost, and I held my coffee closer to my chest as the sweet woman cared for my feet.

After strolling around the airport and having a light meal to pass the time, we finally settled at the appointed gate. Joni located more tour people and started to chat up a storm. I didn't bother joining in. Undoubtedly Joni would share all the details with me later. I took out a new magazine and got lost in unfocused reverie. I looked at the clock and saw we were minutes away from boarding, and I couldn't help dashing over to Starbucks for one last coffee. Joni looked relieved when she saw me come back. Perhaps she thought I had finally given in to my fears and bolted. We boarded the plane silently; we both knew there was no turning back now.

CHAPTER FOUR

It was a cloudy day in Lima. The flight had been long, and my body felt cramped. It was a relief to finally arrive. I did a few inconspicuous stretches as we waited for our luggage. I was confused and tired, so I took solace in the comfort and familiarity of Joni's self-possession and ability to lead the way. Once we had retrieved the luggage, I put on my backpack and followed her to the rendezvous point for the bus that would take us to the hotel. A few of the participants were already seated when we came on. We found a couple of seats near the front, and Joni started chatting with the bus driver in Spanish. She had told me she had done some work in Guatemala, but it did not occur to me she was so fluent in Spanish. I brushed off the discovery. Joni was full of surprises. I put on my sunglasses and tuned everything out.

We finally got to our room in the late afternoon, and I flopped down on my bed, exhausted. Joni did the same, and we just lay there quietly taking it all in. Peru had never been on my radar, and I was pleased I had trusted my instincts and had come this far. Funny how certain life circumstances entice you to do things you would never have imagined, or paid attention to, before. And here I was, in a foreign country, with no idea where the journey would lead me or what purpose it served. I had taken a big risk coming here, and in a moment of lucid inner sight, I felt I was destined to be in Peru.

"We're here!" Joni exclaimed with fire in her voice. "Can you believe it, Carm? We made it! I can take Peru off my bucket list. Well perhaps I should visit it first." She giggled like a girl in a pink tutu. You had to admire her spirit.

"I'm going to have a shower, see how Peruvian water feels on my skin, wash off that sticky travel grub," she declared while stripping in front of me. I guessed this was something I would have to get used to as well.

"Knock yourself out!" I responded as cheerfully as I could muster. "I'll be right here." As soon as the words left my lips, I was fast asleep.

I awoke to a dark room. For a moment, I was completely disoriented until I caught a glimpse of my surroundings. The memories came flooding back, and I remembered; oh yes, Peru. I normally don't nap like that. My mouth was pasty from too much coffee, not enough water, and a long flight. I turned on the bedside table lamp and saw that Joni had left some bottled water, fresh fruit, and a note that read:

> *Gone to explore.*
> *Back in a flash!*
> *P.S. You looked so peaceful, I didn't want to wake you.*

I drank the water greedily, not realizing how dehydrated I was. I looked more closely at the room and noticed travel documents sprawled all over the small table. I spotted a coffee maker with pouches of instant coffee and trudged over sleepily to make myself a cup. It was warm and comforting and didn't taste all that bad. After sipping my coffee, I decided to wash up. The shower revived me, and I felt refreshed. Joni came back into the room moments after I had lain back on my bed. I was eating some fruit.

"Hi, Carm, you're up!" This time she plopped down on the bed right beside me. "Did you have a nice rest?"

I did actually. Surprisingly, I felt so much better. "Yes, thank you. Where did you meander off to?"

Joni stretched like a cat, "I checked out the hotel."

She went ahead and described the facility almost expertly. "There's a really nice market area just a few minutes walk from here. We could go tomorrow morning before the tour group orientation meeting if we wanted."

"But for now, let's rest. Apparently the room service here is divine. You hungry?"

She grabbed a menu from the desk, and I let her order our meal. I was glad not to have to leave the room. The tiredness crept back in faster than I thought.

I slept in. When I looked at the clock, it showed 11:16 a.m. The orientation meeting had started at 11 a.m. I jumped out of bed nearly tripping on the clothes I had left on the floor. Clearly my mind was moving faster than my body. I stood there disoriented, not knowing what to do, until my eyes were drawn to another handwritten note on the bedside table:

Dear Carm. Don't worry!
I'll tell you all about the meeting.
Rest.
Love, Joni xx

I relaxed immediately when I read the note. Where did I find this woman? It seemed like yesterday I had met Joni at the yoga studio. I felt a little intimidated to be taking the advanced classes, and Joni's smile and confident attitude made me feel at ease instantly. There was something about her that was irresistible to me; her authentic and easygoing nature made it simple for me to open up. This was refreshing because I normally kept to myself and focused on my work. Joni was the only person I considered to be a true and loyal friend.

I tried to get up from bed, but my body felt like led. My exhausted and useless state concerned me. Maybe a part of me had no choice but to relax now that I was away from the mess at home. I went back to bed and slept some more.

By the time Joni came back, I was dressed and eating my room service breakfast. I discovered they made decent fresh coffee at the hotel and was already sipping my second cup. Our room had a view of the ocean, and it was spectacular. I was content. I listened as Joni filled me in on the tour news.

It was early morning when we boarded a domestic flight that would take us to a city at the edge of the rainforest. From there, we would go by bus to a port where a boat waited to take us deep into the Amazon. The Lodge we would be staying at was one of the most remote lodges available for tourists. Apparently it was also close to an original Ayahuasca tribe. Joni was really excited about this first leg of the journey, which included a traditional Ayahuasca ceremony. She had been reading about the sacred vine for months, researching it as much as she could. The tour organizers thought it would be best to have the ceremonies at the beginning of the journey before we entered the Sacred Valley and travelled up to the Andes. I made it clear that I would not be participating in any of these weird shenanigans. They weren't my kind of thing, and I had no interest in trying any mind-altering drug or anything of that sort. These things made me nervous and certainly put me out of my comfort zone. I was going to sit this one out, maybe catch up on some sleep or something. Joni gave me one of her "we'll see" looks every time I mentioned I wanted no part in the ceremonies.

It turned out that Maria, the tour guide, was sitting in the seat adjacent to ours and overheard our conversation. She had studied anthropology at university with particular focus on Peru's indigenous tribes. She was obsessed with the traditional culture of her people.

"Don't you know about the Great Ayahuasca?" Maria asked with bright eyes. I shook my head. "Well, let me tell you a story." I could tell she had told this story countless times. I admit, it was riveting. She was a gifted storyteller.

As she was sharing her tale, my mind drifted toward the vast expanse below. I was a little apprehensive about going to the rainforest, not knowing what to expect. I had never been fond of hot and humid weather. My time living in Calgary had given me an appreciation for the mountains, which had begun to feel like home. But flying in the small plane and looking out the window, I could not take my eyes off the rich scenery below. I had never seen anything like it before and was not prepared for it. Miles and miles of greenery so rich and thick I could barely see what moved on the ground. I was totally mesmerized; it was love at first sight. I could not wait to get off the plane and breathe the air and touch the ground. I found my change of heart fascinating.

CHAPTER FIVE

As soon as we stepped out of the plane, we were enveloped in a waft of hot and humid air. Compared to the cooler temperature of coastal Lima, the change was shocking. Joni gasped and smiled at me. We went to retrieve our luggage. Once we'd collected it, we joined the group that had gathered just outside the main doors of the tiny airport. Maria was doing a great job of herding us. I found this amusing and cracked jokes. Joni kept nudging me to be quiet, finding it hard to keep a straight face. As Maria was busy answering some questions, an air-conditioned bus pulled up right in front of the group. In the front window there was a sign that read "The Lodge".

The doors opened and out came a stocky and vibrant Peruvian man. His smile was radiant and made everyone feel instantly welcomed. Maria noticed him and signalled for him to come over.

"Everyone! Gather up here. I want you to meet Felipe."

Felipe nodded and waved. "Felipe is my counterpart in this region. He is the main caretaker of the Lodge and will be our guide in the Amazon. He is here to take us to the port. So gather up!"

On cue we all brought our luggage closer to the bus where Felipe and the bus driver placed it neatly in the under carriage. Joni and I sat near the front of the bus. Joni let me have the window seat and got busy chatting with Felipe in Spanish. Surely she would know his life story within the next hour. It took too much concentration for me to try to figure out what they were saying, so I tuned out once more and stared out the window at the forest wonderland.

I wondered how it would be to be in it, to walk and live and sleep in this great wild place. And I suddenly remembered my intense disdain of bugs and creepy crawlies, for any creature I didn't know and could not have an identifying collar on. Crap! I hadn't thought about that while looking at the greenery from above. Now that I was closer, the reality that I would inevitably meet some unknown creatures made me feel uncomfortable. I nervously checked around my seat to make sure no critter had come into the bus. The coast was clear. I would have to come to terms with this sooner or later, I thought to myself.

An hour later we reached the port and boarded a funky Amazonian speedboat that would take us to the Lodge. It was a three-hour ride, so we settled comfortably in our seats. The excitement in our group was palpable as we made our way up the river, deeper and deeper into the jungle. I began to understand what the hype about the rainforest was all about. I wasn't sure how it related to something spiritual, but this very important ecosystem certainly commanded respect. Its beauty and richness were profound and embracing.

We arrived at the Lodge mid-afternoon. It was a structural oasis in the middle of the jungle, which was built to blend in beautifully with the surrounding environment. Felipe had informed the Lodge of our arrival by radio, and a couple of Lodge employees were already waiting for us by the river. They grabbed the boat with expert hands and tied it to the main dock. Soon after we were all on our way to our dwellings. They were simple huts, very clean, with mosquito nets over each bed. I shared a room with Joni, and we both collapsed on the beds in unison. This time it was me who spoke first.

"Joni! I love this place. There is just something about it. It has me in a trance."

"That's great, Carm! You are such a sport for coming here with me. I am so grateful you did!"

And at that she jumped on my bed and gave me a huge hug. I so loved her warmth and genuine nature. I felt like a cold slice of meat beside her. What a pair we made!

"Want to go for a walk?" Joni exclaimed bouncing off the bed. "Dinner is not for a couple of hours, and we could go explore a little."

"Sure, why not." I was a little stiff from the day's travel. "Movement will be good for me."

I had a mini interior panic attack, not sure what to wear. Would there be bugs? It was too hot to wear pants, so I settled on long shorts, a light shirt, ankle high socks and my running shoes. Joni grabbed a few water bottles and stuffed them in her backpack. She opened a map of the Lodge and laid it on the table.

"Looks like there is a walking trail over here. It's only a couple of kilometres. Want to try it? We should have plenty of time to make it back on time for dinner." I nodded in approval, "Alright, let's go."

We set out like two schoolgirls on a field trip. I was afraid a little but didn't let Joni know. I figured I simply had to deal with my fear of bugs. As we were walking out, we were greeted by some workers who were taking care of the grounds. They waved enthusiastically. Joni told them we were off for a little walk, and they wished us well.

The forest was stunning and inviting. The path was nicely kept and even had interpretation signs along the way. They were in Spanish, and Joni translated them for me. We went along for some time, stopping often to look at new plants and listen to the various sounds coming from the deep green matrix around us. It was wonderful, and clearly Joni was in her element. She must have snapped fifty pictures already. We stopped to look at another marker, and I listened to Joni telling me about the tree it described. It was a rubber tree. As I was looking up at the tree, my vision started to blur, and I felt very dizzy. I grabbed on to Joni to try to stabilize myself, but something felt awfully wrong. Then suddenly everything went dark.

I felt myself lift from my body like a helium balloon drifts up into the air. I was weightless. I became still and hovered about 20 feet above my body. I could clearly see myself lying limp and unconscious on the ground. Joni was frantically trying to figure out what had happened. I could hear her telling me, "Hang in there, Carmen. Hang in there…"

She belted out a shrill cry, "Help! Someone help us!" Then her nursing skills took over. She took off my jewelry, covered me with her blouse, checked my vitals and closely inspected my body to see what could have caused my collapse. I could tell she was worried.

What in the world had happened to me? I couldn't feel any pain. One moment I was feeling well and enjoying my first walk in the Amazon, and the next I felt something was awfully wrong and blacked out. Now I was hovering over my body and witnessing my good friend doing her best to save my life. I was surprised to literally see her prayers for me. They appeared as a bright light around her heart and through the top of her head. I heard her think, "Great Spirit, grace Carmen with your Presence. If something can be done to help her, I know help will come. May your Will be done. Guide me."

She bowed over my body in silent prayer, holding my limp hand in hers. I had no idea Joni had such a deep and rich spiritual faith. She had kept this part of herself well hidden. I wanted to ask her about it. Then a horrific thought descended on me; was I dead? I tried to shout out to Joni, to get her attention and tell her I was alive, but any attempt at communication failed. I started to panic. How could this be possible? What was happening to me? Then my attention was drawn to some movement to the east, and out of the blue a man came dashing out of the thick rainforest. He headed straight to Joni and where my body lay. Joni looked at him in astonished wonder, then relaxed. Somehow she knew this man's appearance was a sign that her prayer had been answered.

The man got to work right away. He scrutinized my body and limbs like a surgeon. He gave the impression he knew what he was doing, and Joni gave him the space he needed to do his work. Suddenly shouts could be heard coming from the trail to the south. Moments later, members of the tour group showed up panting and sweating. Felipe was leading the pack, closely followed by the Lodge medic, who carried a small case adorned with a red cross. As Felipe inspected the scene before him, his eyes rested on the little man caring for me. He was so stunned to see him there, he stopped short in his tracks. He approached more gently and with great respect, making room for the man to continue his work. The group members were asking a bunch of questions, and Felipe signalled them to be quiet. There was an eerie silence as everyone watched.

The little man started to chant, humming in a language I did not understand. It sounded like a cross between Spanish and something else. Then he focused on a spot just above my right ankle and said a name to himself. I saw the reaction on Felipe's and the medic's faces, and their worried looks made me nervous. Experiencing this was making me feel highly uncomfortable, especially since I could not do anything to help myself. All I could do was to continue observing. The man took out a small pouch from his bag. It looked like it was filled with a mixture of herbs. He immediately applied the mixture to the spot on my leg and also put some in my mouth. The medic opened his case and offered a vial to the man; he nodded in approval, although he didn't look convinced it would help. The medic carefully filled a syringe with the contents of the vial. Now Joni jumped to action, instinctively understanding what was going on. She moved me sideways, so the medic could administer the syringe in my glute. How embarrassing.

Then the little man spoke to the medic in Spanish. I recognized a few words, but they spoke too quickly for me to grasp what was being said. They were arguing. The medic kept gesturing towards the path that lead back to the Lodge, and the little man kept shaking his head and pointed forward on the path. The argument went on for a few heated minutes. Joni was watching this in total bewilderment. The little man stopped arguing and gently looked at Joni. He crouched down next to her and took her hands in his. He spoke with her slowly and calmly. By the expression on Joni's face, it seemed that she was grasping what he was trying to communicate. She stood up.

"Let him take her to his village," she said to the medic in a raspy voice. The medic looked at her in shock, but Felipe was intrigued. This time, she spoke more clearly and with authority.

"Let him take her to his Healing Lodge. Now."

She instructed the able-bodied men and women to carry my body and follow the little man.

As my body was lifted and carried, the man paused and looked straight at me. I was stunned. How could he see me? I was floating in mid-air clearly not attached to my body. His eyes pierced my soul, and I heard his thoughts whisper to me, "Go. Go with them. I will guard and protect your body. Go with them." He then got focused and led the way through the forest.

CHAPTER SIX

"Go where? With whom? What was he talking about?" I was utterly puzzled. My attention was drawn towards the light of the sun. I could see waves of light coming through the branches of the forest, brighter than I had ever seen with my physical eyes. Then I started moving in the direction of the light as it became a magnetic force I could not escape. As the current of light carried me forward, I noticed some shapes forming around the light of the sun. Hands and arms extended towards me, calling me closer, and closer, and closer. It felt like I was in an hypnotic trance. I could no longer feel the pull of gravity holding me close to my body and the Earth. The weight of the world below slowly dissipated, along with the scenery, the trauma of my body, the confusion. The sensation was bizarre, like the first moments of anaesthesia when I went for surgery. Yet instead of going into unconsciousness, it felt like I was waking up.

The pull into the radiant disk of light was so strong that I stopped resisting. Somehow it felt familiar, and my fears and worries naturally started to vanish the closer I got to the light. I knew my body was behind me. I knew what I had just witnessed and experienced, and yet, I was not afraid. The warmth of the light entered what was left of me and took me deeper into its embrace. Everything was behind me now. The dense quality of my earthly worries and pains and suffering could not pass through the gateway before me. So I kept letting go. I became lighter. I released. I became brighter. I forgave. I became the radiant light. Moments passed, and I rested in the presence of this light. It was so beautiful, so refreshing, so peaceful. The familiar magnetic pull continued to move me forward and beyond the light. I went through the light disk and saw figures waiting for me.

It was darker once I passed the threshold, and I was surrounded by a backdrop of stars. I recognized some constellations, and others I had never seen before. The stars shimmered brightly. I had a deep recollection that I had been here before. And out of the corner of my eye, I watched a form start taking shape. It was only a vague shimmering light at first. Then as the form came closer, it became clearer. I couldn't believe what I was seeing; it was grandmother!

Here before me was my beloved protector, the kindest person I had ever known. Her brutal death had devastated me, and I had tried not to think about it, to push it as far back in my consciousness as I could. I focused instead on her loving memory, remembering how I cherished the times spent in her genuine presence. I strongly believed that it was her love that kept me from following my mother's alcoholic path. Somehow, I always knew she was watching over me like a guardian angel; and here she was. She looked a lot younger than what I remembered, but I recognized her from a picture of her younger self she used to keep on her dresser in the bedroom. Grandmother was very proud of this picture and told me many stories about it. She was the one greeting me in this unlikely place.

"Welcome, child." She reached for me and gave me a loving hug. "It is so wonderful to see you again. I've waited a long time for this day. Welcome."

I didn't realize how much I had missed her. I started to sob, the revelation of a longing I had no idea lived within me.

"Grandmother!" was all I could muster as I melted into her embrace. We were this way, together, for a long while. I knew that she had passed on many years ago. I didn't understand how we could be reunited like this, so I logically deduced that I must be dead. Or insane. Or that Joni had put some kind of psychedelic in my water bottle. At any rate, I was very confused. Yet the experience felt so real. I could even smell grandmother's aroma, the beloved scent of wood smoke. And she knew so much about me, things I had forgotten about myself. All the precious childhood memories came back to me in an instant. I was shocked to discover I had suppressed these joyful times. Something made me think of my body, and I tried to find it. But I could not see it, or feel it, or get back to it. Grandmother could sense my unease and discomfort.

"There is nothing to be concerned about, my sweet child. You are in this place for a reason. You must trust what will be shown to you. I have come to greet you so you are not afraid. Feel the love and compassion of this place and trust in where it will guide you."

Why was she talking to me in riddles? My rational mind simply could not grasp what was happening to me. I took comfort in knowing that I still had a mind, and a capacity to think and experience. So I couldn't be fully dead, could I? As if reading my thoughts grandmother answered.

"No Carmen, you are not dead. Quite the contrary, you are waking up. It is your destiny. All is happening according to plan. We shall meet again. Go in peace, child. And remember - this is your soul's desire."

And at that, she disappeared back into the aether.

"Grandmother! No! Please don't leave. I have so many questions. I don't know what to do! Come back!"

But she did not come back. I was left in the darkness with her love and blessing to guide me. I guess I should have been grateful for the chance to have seen her again, but I wanted more and did not want the reunion to be over. It was too quick. I did not understand what was happening.

For what seemed like endless moments, I hovered into nothingness. Nothing happened. I tried to follow grandmother, but could not find a way. I tried to return to Earth, to my body, my home, my familiar surroundings, but could not. I was hit by a sense of my life history, remembering the chaos of the last few months, and part of me did not want to return and face the shame. What a mess my life had become. Perhaps being dead was best.

After what felt like an eternity, my life started to show itself in full colour on a screen in front of me. Every single detail of my life appeared, as if moving both at the speed of light and in slow motion at the same time. I was not sure how I could assimilate so much information nor how to describe what was happening. Not one single detail was spared for my viewing. What seemed insignificant to me was shown with great detail and focus. And what was most important to me, like my successful career, barely had air time nor was noticed. The screen was focusing a lot on my relationships, on how I related to and with others. It showed a loving childhood, the times spent learning from my grandmother up until her death. I saw how devastating her death was, not only to me but for my mother and uncle, who both became severe alcoholics. I saw my uncle's lonely death from drug addiction. I understood why my mother had so adamantly rejected her native heritage, for fear of being oppressed, because she wanted to give herself, and especially me, a real chance at success in the world.

I am not sure how it was possible, but I was also seeing my life through other people's eyes and experiences. And this was incredibly humbling. Not one moment of my life was spared; my spirit was being completely torn apart. Very little of what I thought my life was about was real. This realization was devastating.

And the revelations continued. I saw how I had not recovered from the death of my grandmother, and made a conscious choice not to return to my traditional roots because they were too painful. I needed the love of my mother to survive, and she also needed me. I felt a responsibility to her, and I wanted to protect her. How ridiculous of a decree coming from the heart of a ten year old. I saw how this decision had affected so many other decisions in my life. I saw how cutting herself from her roots had led my mother to her severe alcoholism, not the contrary as she thought. I saw the empty relationship between her and my father. I saw how much my father loved my mother and me, although his shy and hard-working personality led us to believe that he was not available to us. I saw how much he tried to guide mother out of her alcoholism, over and over again, pleading with her to embrace her spirit and roots and find joy in her life. But she would not listen and made him the enemy. I saw my father's accidental death, and how he died lonely for the love of his family. For years I had secretly believed my mother that my father was inept at relationships and that he had abandoned her in her darkest times. Clearly this was not the truth. And I felt terrible about it. My entire life had been lived with the belief that men could not truly love. And from that belief an entire sequence of failed relationships followed.

The revelations and the sober witnessing of my life continued. I saw every interaction, every cause and effect, and the impact of my decisions on those I was in relationship with. I saw, and felt, how I had hurt those I loved by being so focused on my work. I saw how meaningless and shallow my life had become, and how my periodic visits to the soup kitchen were a way to keep justifying I was doing something good in the world. In truth, my success was built on the back of others. I had pretended I was indispensable, and people paid me good money for it. I saw how I had wasted thousands of dollars trying to make myself feel better, and that each "success" was but a small fix for my addiction to proving that I was worthy. I saw myself in yoga classes, not doing it for the benefit for my body, mind and soul, but out of insecurity. I did it with no depth. No context. No feeling. It was a means to stay in shape, to keep up with the elite, to make myself feel I was doing something spiritual. I saw how I was isolating myself from my authentic Self through spiritual narcissism. I saw how I judged others for their simple lives, their lack of discipline, their lack of desire to be successful. And of course this judgment came from my own deluded definition of success. I saw them more as a burden to society, that I was righteous enough to carry their passion for success for them.

Worst yet, I saw how hollow I had become. Not the kind of hollow that comes from humility, but the kind of emptiness that comes from the lack of living with spirit, heart and soul. I was like a ghost, an empty shell devoid of original life. I had the foreboding sense that I had missed the mark on my life, that I had it all wrong. And from making one choice at a time that led me further from my Truth, I became denser, heavier, more stuck in my ways. As such, I could see that Larry's betrayal had been inevitable - all the circumstances in my life had led up to it. Castles made of sand, of half-truths, and shallow intentions are made to crumble. That is how it is.

But it wasn't all bad. I was also graced with visions of Beauty. I remembered my early childhood as one of freedom and delight. The best moments of my life were with my grandmother. I shone so brightly when I was with her. I was free of dogmas and false expectations. I was Carmen. I was whole. Parts of me remembered my shining spirit, and that I was part of nature. I remembered that I took solace in nature, in animals, in the wind, the trees and the waters. No part of nature was left undiscovered. The older and successful Carmen had nothing to do with nature, aside from buying the occasional seasonal flower bouquet from the local grocery store. I was shown how adventurous and loving my true nature was. Another part of my life that was shown to me was my tenacity, courage, and resilience. Although I may have missed the mark on my deeper soul's purpose, life had made me strong and gifted me with endurance. I was later to learn that this was the purpose of the first part of my life. I was also to learn what it felt like, and the cause and effect, of living a life out of alignment with the deeper stirrings of the soul.

Then finally, after combing through every inch of my life, the screen went blank. I was thoughtless, speechless, motionless, as if all parts of me were turned upside down, inside out, and scrutinized. This unique review process showed my successes, but they were in no way the major components of my life; they were simply backdrops to the true meaning of my life. What really mattered was how much I had loved, how much compassion I had showed to all sentient beings, and if I was willing to trust in a power greater than myself by letting go of the belief that I had everything under control.

This was the most humbling experience of my life.

CHAPTER SEVEN

I wasn't sure what to do about what I had seen. Was that it? Was my life over? Did I have a chance to make amends? And if so, what would I do? What changes would I make? My heart felt empty. I longed for guidance, for a direction to take, for something that would give meaning and purpose to what I had just experienced.

As soon as I thought this, silhouettes appeared and formed a semi-circle around me on the opposite side of where the cosmic TV screens had been. I was not alone. It was as if I was standing in the middle of a boardroom, being interviewed for the job of a lifetime. I felt embarrassed and intimidated, and didn't know what to do with myself. As my vision adjusted to this new place, I could see the outline of the beings more clearly. Their bodies were much more fluid than the human physical body, and shimmered with some kind of iridescent light.

One of the beings stood up and came closer to me. She introduced herself as Angie, my main life review guide. She welcomed me back as if she knew me. I was puzzled. "Do I know you?" I thought. It seemed like the communication was happening telepathically. How this worked, I did not know. She smiled and pointed to the cosmic TV screen which had reappeared before us. I saw myself standing in a room almost exactly like the one I was experiencing now, but I was the one that looked different. I was in another form and had not incarnated in the life I had just left. I was not sure how I recognized myself, but I simply knew I was looking at "me". The "me" I was observing was excited and keen to be in the process of choosing its upcoming new life. I saw Angie and the same people surrounding her. Together they were looking at similar screens and looking over papers that looked like architectural designs and contracts. The screens and scenes changed often, and we discussed my choices and made decisions together. But the ultimate decisions were mine.

"What is this and what are we doing?" I asked Angie bewildered.

"This is you designing and choosing the main themes and dynamics of your life," she replied as if this was common knowledge.

"Pardon me?" My shock and disbelief were tangible.

"Every soul goes through a process of choosing the main themes and lessons of their lives before they incarnate. You are witnessing yourself making the final preparations, and fine-tuning your current life. You are witnessing yourself as not yet born."

It took me a while to digest this information. There were beings around who were not reincarnating as humans but whose purpose was to assist a soul in choosing an appropriate lifetime that will aid in the growth of their individual soul. I noticed that the beings, including Angie, that were here with me were the same ones that had helped me before I was born. I looked over to the screen again and saw a clear depiction of my parents. I saw their ancestral lineages, their souls' journey, and what major lessons they wanted to work on and learn. I saw there were soul contracts between us, agreements so to speak, to be in loving service to one another's soul missions. Out of the blue I exclaimed, "Is my life over? Have I flunked?"

"No, Carmen. You are not dead. And you cannot flunk at life," Angie was amused.

The contrast between my pre-birth enthusiastic and bright "self" and my current dim state was blatant.

"I look so different now. So bleak, boring and jaded. It looks like failure to me," I was sulking.

"Your life is not over yet, dear Carmen," Angie replied softly with great love and compassion. "Look!"

She directed my attention to the screen. In the frame, I saw myself having this exact conversation with Angie. I saw the room, the review, and my body still in the Amazon rainforest being looked after by Joni and the little man. I was in a coma. My brief time in this place had already made me forget about that.

"I'm alive!" I screamed with surprise and delight.

"Yes. And you were destined to come here," Angie replied.

I saw she was right. An identical moment projected itself on the screen. I saw my bewilderment, the conversations, the life review. It was like watching a mirror image of myself. I had a clear sense there was more to my life story. But the screen did not reveal any information. I asked Angie about it.

"There is more to my life isn't there? Why can I not see it?" I really wanted to know.

"You are shown only what is needed and what is useful for the fulfilment of your soul's purpose," she replied.

I wasn't content with her answer. Why do we forget? How could I have lived my entire life not knowing I had pre-selected certain life experiences? Knowing my thoughts, Angie explained, "Amnesia is a necessary process for human life. First, it is impossible for the human brain and mind to retain and recall the multitude of life experiences over one lifetime, let alone for many lifetimes. Each life is a chance at beginning anew, at evolving. If you knew beforehand the main components of your life, would you still make the same choices?"

I thought that was a good point. If it was destined for Larry to betray me, would I have accepted him as a business partner? "It is not about the partner, or person," Angie continued. "It's about the experience of betrayal. Betrayal is one of the greatest teachers. There are ways that humans learn their lessons, and often it is through the vehicle of suffering. There comes a time when a soul realizes that during the human experience pain may be inevitable, but suffering is optional. This is the mark of a seasoned soul, one who remembers more of their true nature and essence."

I found her last statement interesting. What does it mean that suffering is optional? Is it possible not to suffer? What is the difference between suffering and pain? My mind spun out of control trying to understand this. And I was not sure what to do with the information given to me.

Why was I being shown all of this? And how did one go about choosing life experiences and beginning to remember them if amnesia was such an integral part of the process? Instead of answering questions, this experience had given me so many more. I was bewildered.

It took a bit of time to realize I was not being judged. It was not a test like the ones that made you pass or fail in Earth school. I had a sense there were no right or wrong ways of doing this, and that I was not alone. It seemed that many beings were assigned to look after me, to make sure that I grew as a soul. I could see that the main people in my life, the ones that had been the most loving and the ones that had caused the worst pain, had made an agreement with me before I was even born. It didn't matter if the experience was painful or joyful, there was love fuelling each of the relationships equally.

After all this, I was left with undying questions: How could I begin to change my current life and put it on a more authentic course? How could I remember how to live, to truly live a good life?

And at that, the scene around me started to dissipate. I felt Angie's presence, reassuring me, telling me all was well. An invisible and strong current started to entice me and took me with it. And as fast as I had gotten into this in-between place, I was taken back through the magnetic pull of the current, and back close to my body. It was as if the current knew exactly where my body was. I tried to reach out for the place from whence I came and for Angie, but I couldn't. I was back on planet Earth, entranced by her gravity and the relationship to my body. I had come back home.

CHAPTER EIGHT

I was still disoriented as I re-entered the Earth's gravity field. The magnetic pull to my body was very strong, and I could see myself lying in a small hut in the middle of the rainforest. I knew Joni was near because she was so familiar to me, but I could not see any of the members of the travel group, and didn't recognize anyone else. I had no idea how long I had been away. I tried to look for a calendar, or a clock, or something that would give me an indication of the time and date, but I did not find any clues. Joni looked a little tired, yet happy. She seemed to fit naturally in this place, which was no surprise. Joni had a natural ability to immerse herself within any culture.

In the room, there was a young boy beside my bed. He and Joni were tending after me. I noticed an IV connected to my arm, which looked a little out of place within the remote natural forest setting. I tried to connect with my body, to get back in, to wake up, but I couldn't. It seemed I was still in a coma, yet alive. What now? I even tried to get back up toward the sky, to the place whence I had just come from, but that gateway was closed. I was in some kind of limbo and fully awake within it. It was awkward and unsettling. Yet somehow remnants from my time with grandmother, Angie, and the team of life architects remained with me. I was no longer bound to my fear of death, nor to my fear of living for that matter.

I decided to go further from my body and explore the surroundings. At first, I was reluctant to wander too far from it for fear of drifting and not finding my way back again. So I experimented with going a little further each time but always with my body in view. Then I went further and further, trusting I would find my way back. I realized that simply willing and thinking about being close to my body brought me back there, giving me confidence in this new way of travelling about. What else was I going to do anyway? Every once in a while, I tried my luck and attempted to merge with my body, but it was fruitless. There was no response, as if the doorway had been shut there too.

Once I got the hang of "flying" about, I became more daring. At first, I followed Joni everywhere she went. Her main tasks were to watch over me and care for me. The boy also took part in much of the caregiving, running back and forth, and supplying Joni with what she needed. I saw her care for my leg by removing the bandage, and for the first time, I saw how badly inflamed it was. It looked terrible and badly bruised. Joni gently washed it and put some salve on it, being careful not to be too brusque with it or to raise my leg too high. I tried desperately to make my presence known. I went very close to Joni and even waved my hand directly in front of her face. I shouted, I whispered, but there was no reaction. She could not see me. All my best efforts were in vain. So I tried to communicate with other people in the village. I wandered about, trying to get people's attention, but all they did was continue their daily business, noticing nothing at all. I did, however, get the attention of a small infant. She was lying quietly beside her mother as she was weaving. The little girl would stare directly at me as if mesmerized then break out into a warm smile. I wasn't sure if I was imagining this or if it was really happening, but it was uncanny how this tiny infant instantly knew each time I came close to her. She would even follow me with her little eyes as I experimented with moving around her. She would giggle, and it made my heart melt. At least it was some interaction, I thought. She could not tell anyone that I was present because she had not learned how to speak yet. I would have certainly given her a message to alert others of my presence.

I did not see the little man until the next day. He came back from the forest carrying bags full of plants, herbs, and flowers. His tribe greeted him with great respect and joy when he arrived. At that moment it dawned on me that he must be a medicine man. The small children swarmed around him with delight as soon as they saw him, and he graciously and playfully shooed them away. He went to lay down his loot in a hut close to where my body was. I went closer to inspect what he had brought, and he nonchalantly looked up to where I was and said, "There you are. Welcome back. Did you have a good trip?" And he went about his business.

I was immobilized with shock. After all my attempts at being noticed, this acknowledgement took me by surprise. Once I recovered from the shock, I approached him closer and tried to talk with him, "Can you see me?" But he continued laying out his loot on the table and setting up some plants for drying. So I tried again, "Hum, hello? Can you see me? How come you spoke with me just a moment ago. Hello?" He continued to ignore me. I asked again, this time more annoyed, "Hey Mister! What's going on?" Then he gave me the same gesture he had just used to shoo the children.

I was insulted. How could he do this? I knew he recognized me. But now he was totally ignoring me. This was not a funny joke. I was furious. The little hope I had to figure out what was going on was being toyed with. Did I imagine he communicated with me in the first place? I could swear he was staring straight at me, and I was sure I heard his voice speak clearly in my mind. I was sure I was going crazy. Whatever it was that held my body in a coma, it must have some psychotropic side effects. I was not finding this experience amusing. My guide

Angie had told me it was important to come back and be trusting of what I was going to experience and see. I had trusted her words, and now I felt like a fool for doing so. At any rate, who in the world would believe any of this? This was a strange and cruel nightmare. I tried half-heartedly to communicate with the medicine man again, but to no avail. Feeling defeated, I retreated into the forest.

I wandered in the green landscape feeling more lost than I have ever felt in my life. Certainly, this was a nightmare. I could not eat, or sleep, or touch anything. I was like a ghost drifting aimlessly, yet still being attached to my body by an invisible magnetic force. I found thick underbrush to hide in, and I sulked (if ghosts did such a thing). After a while, I started to pay attention to the noises around me. I had not noticed how alive the forest was. Now I could hear with different ears, and the noise became very loud. It was like a symphony of sounds, a buffet of colours, and scents rich in Earth that permeated the very living space and what was left of my senses. Instead of sulking I started to pay attention to the life around me, and I was amazed. Slowly, I started to explore again. I did not want to return to the village. I did not want to see my body lying helplessly on a straw mat, and I certainly did not want to face the problems facing me. I realized this was the way I had lived most of my life, avoiding what was real and important. My experience in the Other Place had taught me about what I had done wrong but had not indicated ways of how to fix or change my current life. I felt in limbo between life and death, neither here nor there. But at least now I was being honest and candid about it. Was I destined to live like this? Did I have a choice to make? I wished I could have some help with this imposing mystery. I was way out of my comfort zone and did not know where to turn. So I kept paying attention to the forest and the movements of nature. And slowly, the richness of life started to reveal something to me; I was not alone. I was part of the web of life. I started to relax, releasing just a little bit more into this ridiculous experience I felt enslaved to. I had no choice but to accept my current situation. Even my choice to live or die was taken away from me. I could not kill myself, nor could I return to my body. What kind of odd predicament was that? The only logical thing I could think to do was to go check up on my body once more. So I gathered up my courage and returned to the village.

This time I focused more clearly and learned more about what was going on. I noticed that the hut I was in was a little further in the forest, set apart from the main village hub. Closest to the healing lodge was Joni's hut. Half of this hut was set up as guest quarters designed to hold the family members of the sick person, and the other half contained a myriad of plants and medicines. Attached to this were the simple quarters of the young boy. He was the little man's apprentice. He was being taught how to use the plants and how to make medicine, yet mostly it appeared he was like a gopher and servant to the medicine man, running here and there, doing all sorts of menial tasks. I saw the medicine man preparing a herbal salve and the young boy watching intently. I came up closer, wanting to see what they were doing. After a little while, the medicine man asked the boy to fetch some more water. As soon as the boy left the hut, the man looked straight at me, "Oh! You're still here. Are you done sulking in the forest and feeling sorry for yourself?" I was in no mood for insults and didn't try to answer. I just hovered there, not reacting. "I see you've calmed yourself. That is good. Keep observing what you see around you and come back and tell me what you've learned." His voice was commanding but kind.

CHAPTER NINE

I knew better than to doubt the medicine man. Besides, whom could I trust? He was the only living person that had a clue about what was going on. At least he gave me some direction, I thought. So I relaxed into the experience and started to observe what was around me. I could also feel grandmother's encouraging and comforting spirit close to me, and nudging me along. Renewed with a new sense of purpose, I took the medicine man's advice and went deep into relationship with my new Amazonian surroundings.

The village was on the edge of a river. It wasn't very large, yet was teeming with life. Its residents were a practical and frank people who lived almost solely autonomously in the rainforest. There were always activities going on, people engaged in their daily tasks like gathering and preparing food, fetching water, and caring for the children. Unlike my experiences with child rearing in Western society, the children were encouraged to follow the adults around. The children had much more independence and were welcomed in almost any adult activity, and everyone in the community would take great care in teaching them how to work, live, and play. And there was laughter. A lot of laughter.

I meandered further away from the village, exploring the magnificent rainforest. The vegetation was so thick, barely any direct sunlight made it to the ground. I could not 'feel' the moisture and heat because I wasn't exactly in my physical body, but the rich condensation in the soil and foliage indicated it was a very hot and humid day. Even if I could not have possibly been thirsty, my instinct guided me towards a source of fresh water. I found a little stream and followed it aways until I noticed a shape near it, an animal I did not recognize. I was not familiar with the creatures that made this place home, and my curiosity got the best of me. I approached the strange animal as silently as I could. The animal looked like a dog but much more rugged. It had short grey fur, a bushy tail, and rounded ears that looked more like cat ears. I had never seen anything like it. It was drinking from the stream, and as I approached to get a closer look, the animal looked straight at me. I was so bewildered that I ran and hid behind a nearby tree. I must have spooked the animal too because when I peeked from my hiding place, it was gone. I kept looking and noticed that he too had found a hiding place behind a large stone. We stayed like that for a while, and I felt ridiculous. What was I doing hiding behind a tree? Clearly this animal, any animal in fact, could not hurt me.

I remained safely hidden behind my tree for a while longer, not knowing what to do. It was nice to be still, to take in the splendid environment. I relaxed and listened more deeply. And suddenly, a snout was sniffing right next to me. It was the animal, and it had come to inspect me. He was beautiful, and shy at first, but clearly he was at ease. He sensed I was there. I did not know how this was possible, but I knew he felt my presence. I let him sniff around for a bit, while we both got accustomed to one another. Then I tested my theory and extended out my hand close to his nose. And to my surprise, he sniffed my hand directly! He then looked into my eyes and bolted into the bush. The encounter made me smile. It was nice to be recognized. I nicknamed him 'Dog'.

I continued exploring. There were no signs of a city nearby. Only smaller villages existed as I got deeper into the rainforest.

I remembered that the Lodge we came to was at the edge of an ecological preserve. Downstream, I located the Lodge where we had arrived as a group. It didn't seem far away, yet I wasn't sure how long it would take to travel up river by boat to this village, or if there was a trail in the forest that led to the village. There were a few boats in the river tied to docks, and I assumed this was how they had transported me to the healing lodge in the village. I wondered what had happened to the tour participants. I went closer to examine if they were still there, but only vaguely recognized a couple of people. Anyway, the details of the original trip did not matter much anymore, so I continued exploring.

Days passed, and I became more accustomed to my surroundings and the daily habits of the villagers. The village hosted visitors regularly. They came from the surrounding areas to do some trading, socializing, and especially to consult with the medicine man, whom I learned the people called don Luis. Everyone treated him with great honour and respect.

One day, I recognized some visitors as two men I had seen at the Lodge. One of the men, Alphonzo, was don Luis's long time apprentice, and he was the one in charge of conducting the Ayahuasca ceremonies at the Lodge. Sometimes they would talk to one another privately for hours, and one could tell they were very close and had a long-standing friendship. The other man, whom I recognized as Felipe the Lodge caretaker, would spend time in the village, helping out where he could, entertaining the children, and flirting playfully with the elders. He was well received and well loved, and I could tell he felt right at home in the village. I wondered if he had grown up there.

Alphonzo and Felipe would come and check on me regularly and have conversations with Joni. It seemed like Joni had gotten to know them really well. I heard them talk about me and how they were in touch with doctors. They had a tele-phone at the Lodge, and could communicate with a medical team in Lima and gave them updates on my condition. I found it strange that I was kept in the middle of the forest, in a prim-itive setting, in what seemed like a critical "life or death" sit-uation. Couldn't they have taken me to a hospital? Perhaps it was too dangerous to move me. Or maybe Peruvian hospitals were terrible, and this was the best they had to offer. Judging from Joni's behaviour and attitude, she seemed to trust what was happening, and appeared to be in control of the situation, even if I could see subtle lines of stress on her brow. And with her nursing experience, I would have to trust her choice in car-ing for me in these less than ideal conditions, and that I was in good hands. I had no doubt about her competency and was in-finitely grateful for her care.

So in this manner I spent time observing the people and the simplicity of village life. They didn't have much in matter of physical objects, but they were rich beyond compare. Their life was the complete opposite of my life in Canada; I was rich in material goods, but dirt poor in all qualities of humanness and inter-relationships. I was experiencing my total opposite. To top it off, the rich rainforest environment provided an expe-rience I had never had before, one I never knew I would come to love so much.

One day felt a little different. There was a greater than usual influx of visitors to the village, and I was wondering what was going on. There was a taste of excitement and reverence to the air. All day long, the young boy was helping don Luis prepare a certain type of medicine. They brewed it with great care and patience in a large pot on top of a fire. They seemed to be in a deep trance when doing it. Don Luis was praying all day while preparing the mixture, and the boy helped with anything he needed. I recalled Maria saying that the Lodge was close to an original Ayahuasca tribe. Was this where I was being kept? Somehow this made sense to me. I continued to watch the preparations with more interest.

Visitors continued to arrive all day, including Felipe and Alphonzo. No one spoke very much, and everyone looked more contemplative than usual. I noticed that not much food was being consumed either, only simple foods and very small portions of it.

Night came quietly. The moon was full, a perfect time for sacred ceremony. Although the moon light did not pierce through the thick canopy of trees, I could see it clearly in the opening of the river. There was not one cloud in the sky, and even the stars seemed to shine more brightly that usual. A fire was lit in the centre of the village, in the common meeting area. The ones participating in the ceremony were closest to the fire. I remained at the edge of the circle, observing all this. I had never seen anything like it before. I noticed Joni was there as well, preparing to be part of the ceremony. I thought she was courageous to participate. She didn't exude any fear at all, quite the contrary, she was excited and grateful to be part of the ceremony. I hovered closer to her trying to hear what was being said. She was sitting beside Felipe, who had participated in many of these rituals. Don Luis wanted him to speak with her in English to ensure she would not miss any part of the ritual, as it would be offered in Spanish with some ceremonial language, which Felipe was familiar with.

It was time for the ceremony, and the participants entered the communal lodge. The boy took the pot of brew and brought it to don Luis. All the participants were given a cup made of clay, and on it was carved the relief of a snake. I overheard Joni ask Felipe about the cups, and he mentioned they were only used for this ceremony and were quite old.

Around the participants, other villagers were gathered. They made sure the premises were safe, and that the participants were comfortable. They were watchers, so to speak. They looked as though this was completely natural to them, and as if they had done this themselves more than once. This ceremony was an integral part of village life. I was fascinated to witness how sacred and natural it was.

I continued to observe closely as the participants were handed the brew to drink. Shortly after that, Joni started to get very sick, running outside to throw up like she had food poisoning. No one was alarmed, and she received care and help from a woman who never left her side. After a while she stopped having such a strong physical reaction and became relaxed and serene. I could sense the trance state in the air, and I was attracted to it like a moth to a flame. Don Luis was playing his drum, hitting it deliberately and chanting a hypnotic melody. I felt myself drift into the enchanted rhythm. And then I heard his voice in my mind, "This is for you too. You have observed our way of life and have learned much of our physical ways. Now let me introduce you to our spirit." The drumming became all encompassing. "Follow the beat." Boom, boom. "Follow my voice." Boom, boom. "Follow the Great Amaru." Boom, boom. I was too mesmerized and entranced to be afraid. My mind merged with the chanting, and I dissipated into the drumbeat.

CHAPTER TEN

Darkness fell around me. Then the darkness birthed a great big snake with eyes of liquid fire, skin iridescent with starlight, and body moving in unison with the sound of distant drum beats. It looked into me fiercely. I became translucent like the wings of a dragonfly. No place within me could remain hidden from the Great Serpent's gaze. It was searching for Truth and found it deep within me. Then it devoured me.

I was being digested in the belly of the snake. I was not afraid. It felt comforting, and I was astonished. I heard the Great Serpent speak to me in my mind: "I am Amaru, the cosmic giver of life. All life comes through me in birth, regeneration, and death. Not one living creature escapes the journey into and through me." I remained silent, listening intently. "It is one of my kin that gave you that wound." I remembered my leg, how swollen it was, and it all made sense, a snake bite. I didn't know a person could be catapulted in a coma from a snakebite. "The medicine man has slowed down your vitals and heart beat and put you in a semi-trance state, so your body could transmute the poison on its own. If he had not done that, you would have died."

All of a sudden, I became deeply grateful for my predicament. Amaru continued, "I was there in the darkness and observed your experiences in your life review. I have read your heart. You have asked how you can make your life right and how you can learn to live a good life. I want to show you the way to your answers. I am doing this for your benefit but also for all those who are suffering in the same manner as you are. The people of Earth who are my guardians have kept this tradition alive for ages. Now, the common suffering of the planet is affecting not only this long-held tradition, but all of the earth-based traditions our beloved planet has ever hosted. The growing burden of your collective sins is getting heavier and heavier. This is why I have come to you, to reveal to you the truth of what I speak. I am not the best teacher in imparting the Old Ways and dreaming up the future, although I do my best. Let me lead you to the One Who Knows."

I was digesting those words as Amaru was digesting me. As she digested me, I let go of expectations. I became part of her body. And just like the poison from the snake bite threatened to kill me faster if I resisted, I surrendered into a deeper trust in this unique experience. I became very still. Then Amaru began to move on the forest floor. Its slick body undulating on the soft earth. She moved gently and deliberately. Concealed in a thick brush was a large array of stones with a crack among them. Amaru entered the inconspicuous doorway with great ease. It was the entrance to a subterranean tunnel.

Amaru traveled deeper and deeper into the tunnel. The further she moved inside, the warmer it got. As we slid along the pathway, I began to feel a beat pulsing from the ground. It was in harmony with the drumbeat from don Luis' drum, which I could still hear in the distance. The further down we travelled through this tunnel, the warmer it got and the stronger the heart beat became. I was grateful to have the protection of Amaru's body surrounding me, buffering me from the heat and intensity of the pounding heartbeat. After a long time, Amaru slowed down. It felt like we had travelled to the centre of the Earth, and this reminded me of the stories of Jules Verne I had read as a child. In the distance I saw a bright orangey light shining at the end of the tunnel. The tunnel opened into a large cave, and as we got closer, I saw liquid fire at the centre of the cave. I was afraid of it at first, fearing the fire would be too hot. Amaru didn't seem affected by it at all. Although it was hot, it did not burn. She coiled around the central flame to warm herself and rest. She stayed there for quite some time feeling peaceful and exalted. I did not dare to move for fear of disturbing her. So I rested too, yet fully aware of my strange predicament inside the body of a snake.

In my repose I realized the centre fire was emitting a rhythmical beat. It sounded like a giant heart and was no doubt the source of the intense beat that reverberated in the ground during our descent to this place. The sound and pulse were comforting. And for a while it felt like I dozed off, as if sleeping in the loving arms of my mother with my head nestled against her heart. I wanted to stay there forever.

Amaru awoke me from my reverie as she started to uncoil and move again. She went near the entrance of the cave, and in an awkward moment expelled me from her body. I lay on the ground naked, surprised I was in my human form. I could feel my skin, and flesh, and heart beat, and muscles, a luxury sensation I had not been privy to since the accident. I stood up slowly, unsure about my new body. My leg was healthy, with no signs of injury or snakebite. I felt rather exposed standing there naked, unsure about what to do. Out of thin air, a gentle robe covered me up, as if a mysterious force knew about my human prudeness. I was unlike all other animals that lived their entire lives in their own skin. Unless you were a human pet and subject to human whims, no other animal wore clothing. I was grateful to cover up even if I knew I was not being judged. It was habit, I suppose.

The garment was different from any earthly garment I had ever worn or seen. It felt like a second skin and shimmered with a translucent light, even though it was not see-through. I felt incredibly free while wearing it.

My attention was drawn to the central fire as a glow started to emanate from its core. It was faint at first, but started to get stronger with each heart beat. Amaru spoke from the peripheral darkness: "She is coming. Trust her. Go with her. I will be back for you." I tried to speak with the great serpent, but she slithered away further into the cave and disappeared from my sight. I turned around, resolved to experience what was coming next. This journey had been weird, and I was beginning to be more receptive to the unknown. How much weirder could it get? A lot, apparently.

I looked into the fire again. I waited and watched. The energy field emanating from the fire became stronger and stronger until it looked like a large bubble. It grew large enough that it almost touched me. Then I started to feel a pulsing sensation coming from the central fire and up through my bare feet. The pulse travelled up my legs, thighs, pelvis, abdomen, all the way up to and through the top of my head, and further still. It felt delicious and wonderful and familiar. I welcomed the sensation deeper inside myself with each pounding heart beat. Then to my surprise, I saw a bubble forming around me like the one around the fire. When my energy bubble became vibrant, the pulsing stopped and retreated back into the fire. I paused to feel. I took a deep breath in and noticed the larger bubble coming closer to me. With each breath, it came closer, and then all of a sudden it merged with mine. Like two soap bubbles becoming one, I was inside the larger space. The process was seamless. It felt awkward at first, like I was floating around in someone else's body and mind. Yet I retained full awareness of who I was, and my thoughts were still my own. But whose mind was I in? What or whom had I just merged with?

All of a sudden the bubble started to expand. At first it was the size of the cave. Then it went through the earth, as if expanding from an inner central core. It got bigger and bigger until I saw the first water from the deepest part of the ocean. It continued to expand through all the oceans until I started to see and feel the light of the sun. Then it went beyond the ocean and land becoming larger and larger until the bubble reached miles into the atmosphere and encompassed the entire planet. I thought I could touch the moon; it was so close.

Something started to stir from within me. My individual thoughts started to unite with the energy field, and I started to sense a presence that I knew, yet had remained elusive most of my life. I knew deep within my soul I had just merged with the life force and consciousness of Mother Earth.

Everything stood still. I recalled the experience astronauts have named "the overview effect" after looking onto our planet from their spacecraft and seeing it in the backdrop of space. Many of the astronauts reported an overwhelming sense of awe and how small, precious, and fragile the planet looked in the bigger universal picture. None of the words the astronauts used could describe the sensations I was feeling from "being" the planet. I could feel everything as if planet Earth had become my body and my consciousness. There was still a very small part of me that remained, but it was more like background noise than my primary awareness. I knew beyond any doubt a great consciousness was present. I was astonished and humbled. From deep within my heart a gentle voice made itself known:

"I am the Earth Mother. Welcome, child."

Strangely these words reminded me of what grandmother said when she greeted me in the in-between place. I was overwhelmed with emotion. The words were infused with profound love and care. I knew I was safe and that I was experiencing something extraordinary.

"You have been sent to me so I can teach you," said the voice. "It is known you want to learn of the Old Ways. The Old Ways are a crucible of Truth that contain the evolutionary destiny of life on Earth. They contain the Sacred Laws of Life and humanity's purpose and role in the evolution of the Planet. I will help you remember your sacred place in the web of life."

I couldn't believe what I was hearing. It was a poetic language I was not accustomed to. Could I really be in touch with the consciousness of the Earth? Is it really alive? It had always made sense to me that the planet was some sort of living organism. I had never delved into the subject any more than that. If I could trust what I was experiencing, it would lead me to the absolute knowing the planet was in itself a living, conscious being. Up to this point, I had mostly taken the terms "Mother Earth" and "Gaia" as metaphors. My curiosity overcame my shyness and I asked, " Who or what are you? Are you alive?"

"Those are two questions," she replied.

Cheeky, I thought.

"I have been given many names over the millennia: Nature, Mother Earth, Mother, Gaia, in myriad languages, and all of them resonated with the field of truth that lives in the words and reflected the culture of the time. Be aware that I too have evolved over the years. For our purpose, you can call me Mother Earth."

"Why are you called Mother Earth?" I replied innocently, yet instinctively knowing the answer. Mother played along.

"All living creatures on this planet are my children. Without me no life could exist on Earth. You are part of my body, and I am part of yours. Everything you see and experience on Earth as nature has come from me and is me. The sum total of all life forms my body. So in response to your second question; yes, I am alive. I am life as you know and experience it."

It was hard to believe I was having a conversation with Mother Earth while floating in what seemed like an outer space orbit just outside the field of gravity of the planet. I wondered if the others who took the medicine brew were also having a similar experience. Was this the norm? Was communing with Mother Earth a common experience? I wished I had researched the effects of Ayahuasca beforehand and had listened more to Joni. What was I talking about anyway? I was in limbo and did not ingest the brew directly. I was confused.

I hovered in space for a long time. It took a little while to adjust to this new perception. Mother was not saying much, letting me be enveloped by the experience and giving me time to digest the reality of it. I had become part of the Mother's body and mind and was to receive certain teachings that would lead me to live a better life. Maybe being uncomfortable was worth it.

For quite some time, I listened to Mother's heart beat. The more I listened, the more my heart became light, as if it was being purified. My sins, my wrongdoings, the heavy burdens I carried dissipated in her loving rhythmic embrace. It was soothing. As time went on, I thought I would risk speaking with her again. But no words came to my rescue. Only sensations and a great transmission of love. My sensual body was guided to the rocks, the oceans, the trees and countless species of animals. It was so much to take in all at once that my rational mind was forced to take a backseat. Every living creature was connected to a single web of life. Each one had a purpose, a place, and meaning. I found that I could travel in this web, experiencing the life of every creature, from rock to cockroach to killer whale and house cat. Even the most minuscule cell, which could also be broken down into the smallest particles, was part of this web. As I looked up into the dark sky and saw the myriad stars, I wondered if the planet was also connected to a much greater web of life.

"That is not for you to know at the moment, dear one." Mother's voice startled me after such a long period of silence. It was as if she could hear my thoughts.

"I can hear your thoughts," she responded. "We are connected, remember?" That reality still freaked me out. I felt exposed and uncertain.

"You can also know what lies in my heart and soul dear one. The relationship goes both ways."

I hadn't considered this before. It made sense in an odd kind of way. With a quick dose of courage, I let myself drift into a deep knowing and fluid state of mind. And in following this knowing I was attuned to Mother once again. Why were we hovering in space? What was it that she wanted me to learn?

"I want to teach you of the Old Ways. I call them the basic principles of Life. It is my hope these principles will guide you in remembering who you are and your true purpose and place in the world, and also help you lead a better life once you return to your body." I had almost forgotten the mess I had made of my life and my poor body lying in a coma. The thought of going back and fixing everything was daunting. I wasn't convinced it was salvageable. I was determined to give it my best shot.

"That's the spirit," Mother replies with a tinge of amusement.

"So, where do we start?" I was resolved to learn what I must.

"We start at the beginning," she replied confidently.

CHAPTER ELEVEN

"Let me show you how my life began," Mother spoke in a deep rhythmic tone. Before me was a giant cosmic TV screen similar to the one that projected my life review. The current day scene of Earth changed. It became a reflective surface proper for transmitting Mother's memories and story. And she continued:

"In the Beginning was a darkness so grand, it enveloped the entire Universe. The Creator/Creatrix would rest in this vast emptiness and She was content. This space became the backdrop for dreaming and lo! they were beautiful dreams. He dreamt of Creation in all its details. Because the darkness was so deep and the silence so still, the Creator's thoughts were very clear. Because the Creator's heart was good and pure, great compassion infused His dreaming. The dreaming went on for years and years and years. He imagined a creation that would remember this Great Originating Mystery and be bound to it. She imagined all of Creation as part of Her, as one single body. Because He knew not how to judge, all of the created parts were equal in His loving eye.

Then one auspicious day, as the darkness became particularly still, Creatrix knew it was time to release Her Mind Children into the vast empty territory. He took a deep breath, and as He exhaled, He infused all of his creations with his blessings. All that He had dreamed manifested into Being. And in that moment with an explosion of love, Creation was formed. And so was Duality. And the One Mind. And Masculine and

Feminine. In that moment, all that we know, ever have known, and ever will know was revealed. There was perfect harmony.

And He rested for many millions of years.

The Original darkness became self-aware as the years passed. Because Creator had created the manifested universe, Duality now came into being. The Original darkness became the Mother of Creation. She was the dreaming of the Creator's mind. And She too wanted to share in Creation. She and Creator would spend much time together, He the Light, and She the Darkness. They were in Love. And Creator was not lonely any more. The Mother of Creation dreamed of Life, of animating the manifest universe with sentience and meaning. She had stumbled upon the thought of Life. Creator listened to her intently, and one day He wanted to give his great counterpart a present - he wanted her to experience the Life she was dreaming of.

So on another auspicious day, when the darkness was still and the light was bright, Creator called forth the Mother of Creation to be his witness. He then took a deep breath, and together they dreamed Life into Being. This is how sentient beings were born; the birth of the Soul. Now the entire manifested universe was pulsing with Life, vibration, and the desire to return to its divine origin. Meaning was born. And so was Purpose. And there was a great celebration in all of creation.

"Do you think they will remember us?" Darkness asked the Light.

"They are us, my love," replied the Light. "Surely they will know their origin and how they are meant to follow the path home back to us."

For many, many eons the living creation remembered its true nature and origin. All of creation was living in perfect harmony. I was part of this original creation although the Universe as you and I know it looked a lot different back then."

Mother paused in her story. She was deep in thought, and I could sense her nostalgia. I was moved beyond words. She continued in a soft voice, as if revealing something deeply intimate.

"I was created with Love. I am an extension of the Great Mystery and the Light of Creation itself. And because I am Loved, I am Conscious. And in the image of the Original Creation I too am a Mother, the Creatrix of Life. I have been charged with hosting life and living in accordance with the Sacred Laws to maintain, grow and nurture that Life. I wanted this, my Soul was ready for it. I was patient while new parts of creation were born and expanded into our Galaxy, our Milky Way and our Solar System. This took years to manifest. One day, the conditions were perfect for me to fulfill my destiny and purpose - and life on Earth was born."

Then as if watching a very detailed movie on the "Nature of Things", I witnessed a progressive evolution on how planet Earth was formed, how life began, and how it developed, leading to our current time. A few billion years of history seemed like a mere hiccup in the overall evolution of the Universe. And I was only witnessing one tiny portion of the vast array of creation. If I didn't feel small before, this was truly humbling. My rational mind could not grasp the immensity of it.

"I remember clearly when the first human beings were born," Mother mused in a reverie. "My body was already rich in plant life, rocks, animals and water. All were flourishing in perfect harmony. Then Creator and Creatrix came to me in a visitation. We had a habit of communing with one another, and I would share the wonders and blessings of the life I was in charge of carrying. Our minds were not separate. I was part of them and they were part of me. And we would delight in the Beauty of life on Earth because this was one of Creator's original blessings. So we revelled in the Beauty of my body and all was well. Creator and Creatrix told the story of the Origin of Creation often, and I would listen intently each time. It was good to remember. They saw my enthusiasm and an idea came to them simultaneously: what if we made a man and a woman in our image as a reflection of our love for one another? Creator and Creatrix were delighted with the idea. And so, they blew their wish into my spirit, my mind, my heart, my body, my soul; and the first human beings were born.

Even I was astonished. I had given birth to many creatures but none like this. The first humans were of pure Beauty. They were a perfect marriage of the darkness and the light. They carried this truth deep within their Mind, and they remembered that it was through me, Mother Earth, that they were born. They were children of the Earth, and I was so proud. I told them stories of their origin, like they were told to me, and they grew in full remembrance of their cosmic origin as well. They grew into families, then into tribes, then larger communities. They listened to the Earth, and learned the ways of nature and survival. All the creatures accepted the humans well because the human beings listened to them and treated them as equals. Creator and Creatrix were delighted, as was I."

I was deeply moved by Mother's story. My heart was melting, and I didn't know why. It felt like I was listening to the greatest love story ever told.

"Many years passed, and the humans started to think more independently. They started to create larger cities and separation amongst them became more apparent. For many centuries, they relied on a community leader to connect them to spirit and the earth, to their origins. But then, some of the humans started to question if it were necessary to give the Divine Father and Mother credit for the power of creation. They knew the spark of creation was within them, and they started to believe they were better off on their own.

As a result, this created a rift in the human mind and heart. Some humans thought of themselves as superior to the other creatures because they had more intellect and could build things. Instead of using the consciousness graced to them to care for the weak ones, the needy ones, the ones that were sick and in dire need of help, they did not respond. So the rift grew larger and deeper. It created classes amongst the people, illness, suffering, war and premature death. Humans had forgotten the core essential truths of life. And such is the history you are aware of, dear Carmen."

As Mother spoke, her words projected themselves as a living history right before us. It was difficult to watch.

"Once the humans started to turn on one another, they also started to turn on Me." And at that, an entirely different scene started to unfold before my eyes. It showed the devastation caused to the body of the Earth. Every cause had an effect. And over time, the destruction grew like a disease. And the human population grew. And the destruction kept getting greater. The scene stopped at the present day, and the Earth started to spin again at a regular pace. I had just witnessed the last few thousand years of our planetary history. The current history, as I knew it, only formed a tiny portion of the life on Earth. How was it possible to cause so much imbalance in such a short period of time? While watching this, it reminded me of my life review and my time with Angie. I remembered the distinct feeling that I had entirely missed the mark on my life. Could this also be true for humanity? Is humanity missing the mark on its true purpose? The sense of foreboding was too much for me to bear.

At that moment, I felt a deep unity with the Earth Mother. She and I were One united Soul, breathing, pulsing, dreaming, and suffering. All the suffering of the world, our missing the mark on our individual lives and communal lives, was Hers as well. She was our Mother, how could it be otherwise? I could feel her sadness and despair. And for the first time in my life, I truly understood that planet Earth was a living, growing soul in an evolutionary process towards wholeness. My heart was torn apart, and it felt like I had lost my mind.

CHAPTER TWELVE

M other's story of the Beginning of Creation shook me up to the core. Somehow she knew this and gave me time to reflect in quietude and peace.

I had never really delved into anything esoteric before. Discussions on soul, the meaning of life, reincarnation, and life after death were more Joni's territory. I would listen to her speak and get mesmerized by her passion for the subjects. I often had too much on my mind to truly pay attention to her questions and musings, too busy worrying about making clients' houses perfect and making sales quickly and efficiently. Was there truly room for contemplation in a professional world? One could ask questions about the meaning of life, but would they really receive answers? I didn't think so. Up until now, I had sincerely thought that making it to yoga a few times a week was enough of a spiritual foundation. Jogging, yoga, foodie gatherings had become my way of life and an escape mechanism. They were a necessity to uphold the perfect professional image. Just like my houses had to be perfect for sales, I had to exude a perfect image. I realized now how shallow and meaningless my life truly was. This experience with Mother Earth was beginning to nourish my starved spirit and soul.

The realization that planet Earth had a living soul was one of the most profound catalysts of my life. This knowing awakened my heart to a degree I never knew was possible. If the Earth was an evolving being, and we were part of her body, didn't we have a responsibility to her? Or did she have control over us? But that did not make sense. If she had control over us, then surely she would not have let the disharmony continue at this rate and risk the destruction and the health of the entire planet for the sake of one species. She was the primary caregiver of all life on Earth. And just like Creator, she surely did not put one species above another.

"You are correct, Child. I have only a small indirect influence on the choices that humans make. I have made a promise not to interfere, and I have kept my promise," Mother Earth replied. I did not understand. She explained.

"Creator made me promise not to interfere directly with any choices that humans made, nor take revenge on harmful actions. I have been a witnessing bystander to all the acts of cruelty, murder, rape, and destruction. My focus has been on keeping my entire body, mind and soul as harmonious as possible. Up until now, I have managed well and have also witnessed the Beauty of creation unfold. Mountains and rivers, deserts and skies, oceans and forests all thrived in unison for such a long time. So I do my best not to worry too much. But you see, I too am growing and learning as a soul. Although my lifespan is much longer than yours, our desire to be reunited with our Creator by becoming divine beings is the same. It is also within me."

That's what it meant to have a soul, I thought, to have the innate desire to be reunited with the source of creation, to be on an evolutionary path back toward our divine origin, and seek wholeness with creator and with all of creation. And Mother continued:

"I made a promise long ago to honour the sacred contract of free will that human beings have with Creator/Creatrix. No other species on earth has this contract. Although, some species of animals are starting to show signs of evolutionary growth in that area. But for now, human beings are the only ones on this planet that have the choice to live in harmony with the essential laws of Nature and the Universe. Few universal beings have that choice. It is not a matter of better or worse. It is a matter of evolution into light. It also means that human beings have a contract to be co-creators with both Nature (me) and the Universe (Creator/Originating Mystery)."

Woah! That was a lot of information to take in. I wanted to slow things down, so I could better understand what Mother was conveying to me. Soul, free will, evolutionary purpose, co-creative partnership; my mind was spinning. I needed time to digest the new information. Nothing in my life had prepared me for this shift in paradigm. I took some time to be silent and still my mind and heart.

"What exactly does it mean to be co-creators?" I asked Mother from a calmer state. I was ready to understand this. In my mind's eye, I saw a picture of a woman planting a garden. It was as if I were transported to the scene, like programming the holodeck in Star Trek.

"Which other species or life form on this planet do you see growing their own food?" Mother asked.

I searched my memory and turned on my internal sight to scope the earth. I could not find another species. It was a simple question, but I had actually never given it any thought. There were many hunters, but no other species than humans grew their own food. I shared my findings with Mother.

She continued, "Exactly. And how many other living beings manipulate or change the natural environment to meet their needs?"

And as if on perfect cue, the woman in my "vision" picked up a clay pot that she had made from the earth and made her way to a watering hole that had been created by damming a part of a stream with a few stones. It wasn't a large dam, just enough to make a larger pool of water for easy access. She kneeled down close to the earth and filled the container with water. All the while she was collecting the water, she sang a little song of praise for it, thanking the water for its generosity and explaining how she is helping the seeds in her garden grow into food that will sustain her family. She returned joyfully to her plot of land to nourish the freshly planted seeds.

"I see. Only humans change the environment to suit their needs." This seemed clear to me. I wondered if I had missed anything.

Mother continued, "Changing the environment to suit ones needs is an essential and natural part of nature. A beaver who builds its home or a bird that builds its nest does it in partnership with the world around them. It is a movement forward, a procreation, a natural expansion of the species. Every living creature plays its equal part, from the lowliest single cell life forms to the most sophisticated predators, all play a role in the Great Web of Life. But none of those creatures manipulate the environment to take more than what is needed."

The scene with the woman and her garden changed. She went up to the stream to fetch water and found it had stopped flowing. She wondered what may have caused this and followed the rocky stream bed up towards its source. A while later she reached a large stone wall that redirected the stream into a large pond. She wondered who had done this and went to the pond to inspect. The land belonged to a neighbour, and because it had been a dry year, he had taken it upon himself to collect all the water he could, so that his crops would not die from drought.

The woman saw the man near by and approached him, "Kind Sir, why have you blocked the stream?" she asked politely.

"Why Madam, so I could water my crops of course."

The old man had many crops, which he sold at a high price at the market. The woman knew it was a dry year with little rain. She had been taught by her mother and grandmother about the cycles of the earth, and that there were years when the stream would flow less abundantly. She was taught to be diligent and aware and never use more than what was necessary. This way the health of the stream would recover when the time was right. One needed to be patient.

She openheartedly shared this knowledge with the man, mentioning that so much life depended on the water down stream, and there were plenty to share if we did it the way it had been taught for generations. The old man looked at her and said nothing for a while. Then with an eerie laugh he said:

"Those methods are useless. Times have changed, you ignorant woman! I can take as much water as I want because that is what I want. And if I see you or your kin coming to steal some of my water, I will let everyone know you are a thief, and you will pay a big price. I hope never to see you wandering on my property again."

The woman picked up her gourd and left. She wished that her tears were enough to fill up the river bed, but alas they were not.

The scene went dark again. I simply could not speak. The grief in my heart was intense with a sadness so profound I too could have filled that stream with tears. Why did this witnessing move me so much?

Mother did not have to say a thing. I understood what she wanted to convey in her story. As human beings, we have the power to both create and destroy. And there is a distinction between using this power for the health of the whole or for personal gain. Being a co-creator demanded great responsibility, leadership, compassion, and steadfastness. It meant being willing to share and never taking more than what is needed. When this fine balance between giving and receiving gets disturbed, suffering occurs. And this creates even more imbalance. The woman in the visionary story had learned from her tribe how to honor the Earth, and listen to and work with the natural cycles of life. This is how they knew the stream was dryer some years and very abundant during others. And the animals and plants would know about these cycles as well. And the humans and the plants and animals and rocks and elements would communicate with one another. And they would remember to live with one another and help each other when needed. One would never hoard what another needed for survival. This simply did not happen. It was inconceivable. I turned my attention to Mother.

"Is this what being a co-creator means, Mother? To work in harmony with all of the forces of life and to give them a voice and place in what you do. And to always keep their well-being in mind and heart when creating," I hoped my explanation made sense.

"Yes, Child. You are starting to understand, but you are forgetting an important part. Let me show you."

The darkness revealed a familiar scene. It was the creation story Mother had shared previously. I remembered the Love that Creator and Creatrix dreamed into Creation. I remembered that human beings were not only Children of the Earth but Children of the Stars as well. And we had the spark of divinity within us.

"Good," Mother responded. "And would a child born of this immense Love, who has been given the power of creation, use it to stop the flow of evolution or to help it grow towards its greater purpose?"

This was a big question, but I believed I understood. We have the power to create because it has been gifted to us. If we hold on to this gift and don't pass it on, it becomes stagnant, and that part of the web of life cannot thrive. We are meant to pass it forward for the benefit of all of creation and all sentient beings in creation. That is how it works. That is how it is. Co-creative partnership means to work with nature. Nature serves us, but we also serve her. This is a sacred relationship. This is what building a relationship of trust with the seen and unseen forces that make up the world is all about.

"Let me show you something," Mother said kindly. She was enjoying this process. And I was keen to learn some more.

The scene came alive once more. It was nighttime, and the stars were shining bright. A group of people were gathered around a fire. The woman from the previous scenes was there, sharing with her community what had happened at the stream bed and with the neighbour. Everyone listened attentively, giving her the space she needed to confess her feelings about what had happened. Her Grandmother was present and was listening very attentively. She then began to speak:

"What I had feared has come," she said. "Long have I listened to the trees and the birds, and the waters and the sky. And they told me of the ones who would use nature for their own benefit and forget to live in harmony with the land and all our relations. It has been foreseen, this illness of mind and heart will spread like a disease and become the weight of the world. That is what the prophecies say, when one becomes still and listens."

She paused, deep in thought. She shook her head as if to get herself out of a trance and gave her granddaughter a warm smile, "But for now child, let us ask for guidance about what to do about water. The village needs water or else we risk great danger of thirst. So let us ask our allies for help and ask the water spirits for direction. This is what you do."

The wise old woman fell on her knees and prayed to all the directions. She offered gifts to the fire, food and herbs and flowers. She enlisted the help of her ancestors and all the invisible forces that always came to her aid, whenever they were asked. She then took a small clay bowl with water in it and passed it to everyone gathered there. Each person held the cup gently in their hands, offered their intentions and thanks, and passed it on to the next person. The woman was last and passed it back to her grandmother.

Once the old woman received the cup, she offered it up to the sky. Then she laid it on a smooth rock near the fire. She instructed her granddaughter to come near. "This cup and water are empowered with the loving intentions of the tribe. Our needs have been spoken. Now the fire will bring an answer, because all prayers are heard and fulfilled by the Great Mystery. So sit child, be still, and listen."

The woman looked visibly awkward, but her heart was full of love, and her intentions were pure. She was learning the Old Ways and was being passed on a divination method practiced by her people for generations. One day people will come to her for guidance, just like they come now to her grandmother. So she looked into the fire and became like a hollow reed. She let her mind free and let go of expectations. The fire, dancing in the moonlight, put her in a slight trance. The people were drumming, softly at first, then more intensely and deliberately. She then got up and started to dance and move around the fire. Just in the corner of her eye, she saw a small bird hovering behind the people, getting her attention. She was mesmerized by this bird and followed it. She went a little ways and stopped at a location. The little bird spoke to her in her mind, "If you dig here, you will find water. It will be an abundant spring and will not run dry. May it serve your people well." Then the little bird spiralled towards the heavens and disappeared from sight.

When the woman came back from her trance, she was still sitting on the spot shown to her by the little bird. She ripped a piece of her clothing, wrapped it around a tree nearby, and placed a beautiful stone where the bird had landed. She heard the drumming again and noticed there was light appearing in the east. As soon as she stepped near the fire and her people, the first ray of dawn came upon the Earth. Her grandmother smiled knowingly at her, "What do you have to share with us?" And the woman shared what had happened with the little bird and what it had told her. The people listened gratefully and were at peace. Everyone went to sleep.

A few hours later when everyone had rested, the woman found the place the little bird had shown her. She showed her people the spot, and they started to dig. They sang songs, and after a short while, there was an exclamation of joy - water was coming through the bottom of the hole. They dug further and soon the hole filled with beautiful, clean water. They had discovered an underground source. There was a great celebration that night. The people would not starve.

The scene went dark. I was so enthralled by the story that I had forgotten I was having a conversation with Mother Earth and that she was teaching me about co-creation. Although this was something I had not directly experienced in my life, it made much sense to me. But for the woman in the vision, it was part of her daily life. When one had a reverent and respectful relationship with Nature and the Great Spirit, they always provided. As human beings, we may have a certain kind of intelligence, yet that does not make us any wiser than any other living creatures that naturally know how to live in harmony with nature and life.

Much wisdom is gained by learning to co-create. It is our responsibility to create wisely. It is our responsibility to ensure the balance of life is sustained while we create. It is our responsibility to provide for those who need our help, just like they help us when we need theirs. Today for you, tomorrow for me. This is how it is.

"I am proud of you, Carmen." I could sense Mother holding me closer in her embrace. "You are learning well. Your heart is pure and your courage a great strength. Thank you for listening. Thank you for coming here. Thank you for helping me remember who I am. Thank you for remembering me."

"Sacred Mother," I answered. "It is I who must thank you. I was living a life that was empty. You are showing me how to live. You are helping me remember my true nature. It is I who is indebted to you. There is nothing I can give to you that you have not already given me a thousand fold. And for this, I bow to you." I was filled with reverence deep to my core.

"Now you understand, sweet Carmen. Now you understand the essence of co-creation and sacred reciprocity."

I was too humbled to reply.

CHAPTER THIRTEEN

I now understood that to be a co-creator in the Great Work one must develop sacred relationship with both the natural world and the world of spirit. I wondered why the woman in the story knew and understood this and the man up river did not. What made one person act one way and another the opposite?

"Life is filled with duality and polarity," Mother responded. "Sun and moon, day and night, birth and death, creation and destruction, all of these aspects of creation and reality are no better or worse, good or bad. Each has a role to play in the overall balance of life. When one aspect is chosen repeatedly over another, it creates disharmony and affects the whole."

I had realized by now that Mother liked to teach through stories and visions, and the screen in front of me changed again. This was the best version of the holodeck one could imagine. Mother would rock at a Star Trek convention, I thought, but I digress.

Before me were a couple of children at play. They had made a natural scale from a flat piece of wood balancing over a centre stone. It looked like a smaller version of a seesaw. The game started by choosing two equal sized stones, which both children would place at the same time on each end of the wooden board. This would ensure it would not tip over too much to one side. If the board touched the ground, the game reset. The goal was to place an object on each side of the plank at the same time, to eventually have as many objects as possible held in balance on each side. They would count how many turns they'd had and did their best to get a better result every time. The game allowed the participants to cooperate with one another and learn the Law of Equilibrium. I noticed how joyful the children were and how much attention they paid to the game. Many others came to watch and encourage and went to gather all kinds of natural artifacts to place on the scale. A small child caught a couple of chicks and the children tried to keep them both on each end, which was futile and hilarious. I was amused watching the children play.

Along came a tall child, who was from a faraway village, whose land had become too dry to live on. His family was in search of new land to settle on. He was not familiar with the game and did not try to understand it. Without notice, he picked up a large heavy stone and placed it on one side of the plank. Instantly the plank hit the ground sending all the opposing objects flying in the air. The playing children were shocked, and so was the tall child. He did not understand why the other children did not think he was smart. He had won the game and felt proud that he had outsmarted the others. The adults were drawn to the commotion and came closer to investigate. One of the children explained what had happened. The adults spoke amongst themselves, and then one of them spoke to the children. I could not hear what was said.

There was a long pause. I was sure there would be some form of action from the adults or from the children towards the new boy's behaviour, but there was none. The children simply resumed their play as if nothing had happened. The boy stood there in disbelief and went over to pick up another large stone. But before he could put it on again, all the children stopped doing what they were doing and looked directly at him. They did not provoke him or prevented him from placing the stone on the plank again. They were still and just waited to see what would happen. The boy stopped dead in his tracks. He stood with the heavy rock in his arms, and slowly, his mischievous smile turned into a frown. He could not understand why no one moved or tried to stop him, since they had been visibly upset when he had done it the last time. He stood there so long that the rock became very heavy, and his arms started to hurt. He finally dropped the rock and ran into the forest. The children joyfully resumed playing their game.

"What was this game they were playing?" I asked Mother, not totally seeing the point of what she had showed me. I understood that the children were learning about balance and were playing a cooperative role with one another. It was unlike any of the games I had grown up with, save perhaps Twister, and surely very different from the multitude of video games played these days. What did strike me as unusual was the reaction of the children when the boy had come back again.

"That is a good observation," said Mother. "Why do you think the boy did not act?"

I pondered the question. I thought of a martial arts movie I had seen, where the master was trying to teach his student about non-fight and the mastery of his tradition. The student did not understand why he should not fight because he received great admiration and power when he engaged in fights. He was very good and won most of his battles. The more he fought, the better he became, and his thirst for winning became stronger after each fight. One day, he believed he was stronger than his master and provoked him to fight to determine who was strongest. The master kept refusing to fight his beloved student. His refusals frustrated the young man so much, that one day he could not help himself and decided to take on his master dead on. The look of betrayal on the masters face was unmistakable. When it was clear that his beloved student would not back down, he became empty of desire and did not move. As the student prepared to strike his master, an invisible force took control, and all of the student's power was turned against him. He was struck down with an invisible force that left him breathless. His master had not moved at all."

This time, it was Mother Earth who listened to my story attentively. She had not heard this story before, it seemed. I was no martial artist but did my best to relay what I remembered to Mother:

"Once the student regained his senses, his master explained. His words were filled with compassion. "There is no enemy," the Master said. "There is only yourself. The outer world is only an illusion. The more you make enemies and perceive yourself as different, the more you become like them until the very thing you hate and fight consumes you. There is no difference between the fighters, only what they fight for. Protector and destroyer are but the same. When one begins to understand the futility of the fight, one becomes unattached to the outcome, releasing the need to win and letting a higher power take over."

The student did not like what his master was trying to teach him and refused to continue his lessons. He kept fighting on his own accord and with his own rules. One day, after many battles, the student finally looked at himself in the mirror and was appalled at his reflection. He had become what he had most feared. In that moment, he repented, and finally understood what his Master had been teaching him all these years. You become what you hate, and you become what you fear.

He was finally ready to face his greatest enemy. He had been preparing for this all his life. All the hard work, dedication, and focus would finally pay off. The community would finally find out who was the best warrior in the land. It was a fierce and brutal fight, with both men equally strong and equally powerful. After some time neither side showed more weakness or strength than the other. The student had enough of the fighting. He knew he was fighting himself and that his opponent was just as worthy to live as he was. He understood that life did not choose one to be more worthy than the other. So he became still, took a deep breath, and put his sword vertically before him. This was a sign of surrender. Then the unexplained happened. Just as his enemy saw the opportunity of defeating his rival and stepped closer to deliver the final blow, his sword hit a kind of invisible field which catapulted him backwards with tremendous force. He looked at his sword, and it vaporized in his hands as if it had been soaked in a powerful acid. He was stunned. He was sitting on his buttocks and could not move. He looked up at his opponent with terror and inquisition, wondering what he would do now that he was defenceless. He lowered his head and welcomed defeat and death. The student came out of what seemed to be a deep prayerful stance, looked into the soul of the warrior on his knees before him, and knew right there and then there are never any winners in a fight. And he walked away."

When I stopped, the screen became dark. I was surprised that the story I told became alive on the cosmic screen just like the ones Mother had shared. I thought about this and why that was. It seemed that thoughts became very active in this place, and I was learning to communicate with the soul of the Earth. I was so used to the verbal communication on Earth that it did not dawn on me that another more efficient form of communication could exist. With all the different languages in the world, wouldn't it make sense to have a universal language that did not rely on "words" but more on thoughts, sensations, feelings and vibration? It made me wonder if this was nature's language. How else would we communicate but through the heart? The heart knows no boundaries, and it does not judge. This was what the martial arts student in my story was learning about; the universal language of nature and the power that holds each life sacred.

I sensed Mother's silence and deep contemplative state.

"I like martial arts," she finally said. "I like how you describe them in that way. They were originally created to teach humans about the ways of nature, living in harmony with the elemental forces of earth, water, air, fire and aether. They were also created to help vitalize the body and make humans stronger, wiser, and more powerful as co-creators. All original forms of martial arts were neither offensive nor defensive. There was no need for that. Only training for greater harmony and balance. They were created to strengthen the power and unison of the essential elements within the body and within the movements of nature. To this day, you see remnants of this ancient and primordial teaching of life, yet most have been distorted or forgotten. Some do remember and practice, and it takes years to master. The Old Ways are to be found in the very essence and practice of these arts. You have been given a glimpse into the Universal Law of Polarity. Remember it."

I was surprised I was having a conversation about martial arts with Mother Earth. And I was still reflecting on how precious it was that Mother and I understood one another so well and about her teaching methods.

"I speak in ways that you will understand most clearly, dear Carmen," Mother Earth continued. "Every era has its own personality and sets of challenges, every time its own elements that form its experience and environment. It is important to talk about and use examples that you can relate to, that are appropriate for you. You are a woman of the twenty-first century, of a time where population and technology have never been more prolific. No other age in human history has been like this. This is the time of the Great Turning, as prophesied by the visionaries and mystics of the world."

"The Great Turning?" I repeated, not sure what it meant.

"We will get into that if the time permits," she replied. "Our time is limited and there are still important wisdoms I want to remind you of."

CHAPTER FOURTEEN

Even in this peaceful place between worlds, my fears and anxieties found me. Flashes of memories came flooding back: being betrayed by Larry, my life crumbling down, the trip to Peru, getting to the Amazon, the snakebite, meeting grandmother and my council, not being able to return to my body, learning about village life, being present at a ceremony, and being catapulted to the centre of the Earth by Amaru, the great serpent spirit. And now, having a full on holodeck conversation with Mother Earth that felt so real that I had momentarily forgotten about my life. Good grief - had I totally lost my mind? I was seriously concerned about my mental health.

"Fear not, little one," Mother cajoled, amused by my thoughts. "It is true you've had many experiences in the last weeks that have revolutionized your perception of reality." More like, blew whatever was left of me apart like an atomic bomb, I thought.

She continued unfazed, "One must be taken apart and purged in order to let in a new reality. What you were must be destroyed, so your authentic Self can emerge. This is often how it is done. At times the experiences are so extreme that you have no choice but to enter the Cloud of Unknowing and release all that you thought you were."

That was putting it mildly, I thought, feeling desperately sorry for myself all of a sudden. No one would believe me, and I felt very lonely. Even with all the beautiful experiences I still did not understand why they were happening to me.

"Now you can appreciate why amnesia is a safety mechanism for the human mind," Mother remarked. I remembered what Angie had told me about spiritual amnesia when we are born. I was now convinced that ignorance of these matters had its strong points.

"Growing a soul is about remembering," said Mother in a distant and almost sad voice. Then a thought entered my mind and I gasped, "Mother! You have a soul too. Do you follow the same rules, or laws, as the human souls?" I waited earnestly for an answer.

"Yes of course," she gently replied. "All living sentient beings follow the same laws. Including me."

"Does this mean that you too have amnesia?" I asked.

"I was not designed that way. I remember, but human beings have forgotten about sacred relationship and reciprocity. All of nature remembers without knowing. Yet for the past while, humans have veered away from the universal laws and have created much confusion, strife, war, and illness. This heaviness affects me. It has become my burden to bear. You and I are not separate - what is yours is mine. And what is mine, is yours. And through your forgetting, I too have begun to forget. And this is not my wish. I cannot, will not, stray from my divine expression and purpose." There was a long pause.

"So what will become of us, of humanity?" I asked with fear in my heart.

"I do not know. I do not know all of Creator's plan. I do know that my purpose is to keep balance. And that all balance has a limit and has a tipping point. This is what is referred to as the Great Turning," she paused for a moment as if to let me take it all in.

"My position is clear. I love my children more than you can imagine. My purpose is to create, nurture, and regenerate life. Death and destruction are also part of who I am, yet I do not have the power to decide which species continues to thrive and which becomes extinct. They do that themselves, through cause and effect, with their choices to live in harmony or disharmony. Sometimes, a species goes extinct due to evolution, and this is part of the greater process of life. Just like prey will surrender itself to a predator because it is ill or old. It does this for the protection of its species and survival, not only for themselves, but for the health of the whole. Sometimes, a species goes extinct for the benefit of the greater good. Times are different now. Much of Humanity has changed the rules of life. The Old Ways state to only take what is necessary - all animals, plants, and elements knew this. It was an honor to offer oneself for the greater good. An antelope gracefully offered its life for his fellow brothers and sisters. And the one who took a life prayed for the spirit of the prey, in full gratitude, thanking it for its sacrifice. And the prey became part of its spirit, part of the living matrix of life. These were the Old Ways. And it was the animals that taught these ways to the humans. And the humans listened, and all was well." Mother fell silent, contemplating what she was remembering. She continued:

"Now it is different. Humans have gotten into a habit of taking more than necessary and have forgotten to give thanks for the sacrifice of the life that nourishes and sustains them. I am the life. I am the sustainer. It is I that you forget about when you stray from your original purpose as loving co-creators. It is me you have forgotten."

I felt terrible. She was right, there were little remnants of the Old Ways she spoke of in my life. I had seen the movie Avatar, and it reminded me of what Mother was speaking of. But aside from that, where were the sacred truths of life to be found? In my recycling bin? Surely that was not enough to give back. Where had the true role models gone - on a Hollywood movie screen? If I could have had a panic attack in my spirit body, I would have. The situation felt way too daunting. I had to ask:

"How are we to remember you, beloved Mother? How can we begin to give back what you have given us, even if nothing could match your generosity?" The words blurted out of me like I was holding on for dear life. Well, actually, I was in a way. Maybe this was one of the reasons why I was given this chance to see how I missed the mark in my life, to remember my purpose and have a chance to manifest what is true. And I was convinced that restoring a loving relationship with Mother Earth was an essential part of living a good and authentic life. I repeated gently and earnestly, "Mother, how shall I begin to restore what is sacred in my life?"

"By loving me, dear Carmen. By remembering that you and I are the same. That all living creatures are the same. So treat them as your equal and never take more than what you need. And when you have been graced by abundance, share in your bounty. I am not talking about acts of charity that hold no responsibility. Money does not equal abundance. Money does not restore harmony in the world. It is a commodity, nothing more, nothing less. And in a culture that puts money in a place higher than the sacred, it becomes too personal. One loses the essence of Beauty that money carries within its soul. By having desire that is not discerned by the heart, one creates an output that the heart and mind and body cannot keep up with. The largest debt human beings can accumulate is an unfulfilled life, a life that does not honour and fulfill their soul's contract."

It seemed odd to me that the topic of money came up, especially when asking about giving back what is given so abundantly. Perhaps that was why; maybe my thoughts of giving are so intertwined with the philosophy of money. Most giving and receiving is established through a money exchange. It is so ingrained in my culture that it is pretty much impossible to detach from it.

"Good, child," Mother resumed. "I wanted you to make the connection because of your already abundant experience with giving and receiving. When you are in the flow, everything feels like it is running better. And this empowers you." True, I thought. I'd experienced great flow and elation when I was at the top of my game in my career. Perhaps this was why I wanted to keep it that way, to keep returning to it like an athlete seeks out the "zone".

"Exactly," Mother responded. "What I want you to start practicing is the art of giving of yourself. This giving has no cost, but is priceless. It is about being grateful for who you are and exactly where you are at. It is about transmuting and letting go of what no longer serves you, what you have outgrown, what keeps you suffering, and what makes others suffer because of you. As you release what does not authentically belong to you, you help re-member yourself. When you re-member yourself, you re-member me."

Her words did not fully make sense to me. I didn't grasp what Mother was saying and how it applied to my life.

"Let me show you," She responded.

A familiar scene appeared before us. It was Larry and I having an argument over shady legal documents that a lawyer friend of his had drafted for a client. I had a bad feeling about it and knew something was amiss. I asked pointed questions that made Larry very reactive. I was so focused on "being right" that I negated to address the legal issue that was right before my eyes. I knew something was off, and I didn't have the backbone to say anything about it for fear of losing face and showing lack of support for my business partner.

As it turned out, this false transaction was the first of many that Larry accrued over the years. And I knew something was wrong, but I did not want to believe it. To uncover the truth would have forced me to deal with it, and I would have risked losing everything. I hoped it would work itself out on its own. So I stuck my head in the sand, deeper and deeper and deeper. I was not being honest with myself, and I did not have the courage to follow through on my intuition and instincts. I was too afraid to lose the prestige I had. This created disharmony. It created heaviness in my soul. It created the perfect environment for the ugliness to breed and continue and for my castle made of sand to come tumbling down.

With this, I realized I was being greedy by not confronting Larry about his unethical business practices. His values did not match mine, and by my accepting his, it resulted in influencing the business in ways that brought it further away from my own sense of integrity. Larry's set of values became part of the business, and I was denying it. When they were allowed to take root in the business, they also became part of me. So in a way, I had betrayed myself. There was no one to blame but me. I had not been generous with giving of myself, instead I had held back on telling and confronting the truth. And I had paid dearly for it.

Mother became very still and quiet, giving me the space to contemplate my thoughts.

CHAPTER FIFTEEN

So I had a part to play in the fiasco that happened in my life. I tried to cover up lies, and even though I was not directly involved in the actions of stealing, my greed and obsession with success had blinded me to what was real. My world had no choice but to tumble down because it was founded on lies and denial. And I was willing to bet that was not the only instance I had betrayed myself.

What had made me the way I was? I was a happy child, especially while living with grandmother. Being with Mother Earth made me realize that so much of my ancestral blood had been denied within me, and that it desired to be freed. I recognized that so much of what Mother had been telling me, grandmother was also teaching me in her own way, especially with her passion for canoe making. As she worked she would tell stories. Stories her grandmother had told her, stories she would sometimes make up right on the spot with a cue from nature. These were teaching stories. I see now how connected to nature she had been, and that she had learned and practiced the Universal Language. Mother began to teach again.

"The Universal Language is one born of stillness and silence. It is one that all living creatures know in their hearts, as a seed of remembering planted by Creator/Creatrix. No human language can ever contain it fully. Some cultures claim their language is the closest to it, but no human language can encompass it fully. To understand and start to know the Universal Language, one must first be devoid of words."

The scene changed before me. I floated into space, far away from where I had been near planet Earth. A magnetism carried me on an invisible wave, and it seemed I was travelling inside a wormhole through time. I was not sure how far I went, but the solar system and the Milky Way Galaxy passed by my vision in a flash. I saw star systems and galaxies and nebulae and countless other phenomena pass by me in mere seconds until I came to an abrupt stop. It was as if I was at the edge of the Universe; and it had no beginning, no end. No form, only potential. And from within the darkness a still small voice could be heard. It was the voice of Mother Earth, "Here, at the beginning of time, is where the Universal Language originates. Listen to the vast silence. Be still and listen."

So I dropped everything. I became as dark as the stillness, as open as the silence. And then I felt something. It was a pulse, a rhythm, a vibration of pure light. I did not breathe, it was breathing me. It took hold of me, and I merged with it completely and seamlessly. I do not know how to describe this expansive state - the best way I can define it was one of pure unbounded Love. And I saw coming out of this Love an immense web of Light. This web looked like a giant flower, connecting all that I had seen on my way to this place. It was magnificent as it shone. And what travelled through this web that linked all of creation was the Universal Language. I paused to cherish this moment and take in and remember as much as I could. My rational mind was not equipped to understand this. It would be simplistic to call the Universal Language the Language of Love and the Heart, but frankly, that is what I felt it was. There was no other way my human mind could describe it. It was an unspoken language; one that had reverence for all of creation embedded in its very essence; one that honoured every part of creation as equal; one that continually strived to bring balance and harmony to Creation. And it was born from Love. That was the original impulse. Love was the Universal Language. I simply knew this to be true. I couldn't explain it, I simply knew.

And in a flash, as if waking from a dream, I returned to the place Mother and I were having our conversation. I was calm and peaceful.

"Now do you understand?" Mother asked inquisitively.

I did not respond with words. I remained silent and still. I communed with Her, in my heart, from my soul, and felt her Being, and her Truth, and her Purpose. And I knew she felt mine. We were both alive. We were both on an evolutionary journey. We were both born of the same original thought. Great love came over me, and I bowed to Her. And in return, She bowed to me. No words were needed to share this deep knowing and respect. The Great Mystery lived in her as it lived in me. And we held one another in the sacred and tender space of our knowing.

"You are a good dancer, dear Carmen." She said to me joyously.

"And so are you, Beloved Mother. So are you."

Nothing else needed to be said. We remained in silence, sensing one another, Being with each other.

When I came to a more ordinary consciousness, I looked onto planet Earth and wondered how the Universal Language manifested there. Instantly, an image of migrating birds came to my mind's eye. The wind spoke with them when it became stronger and changed directions; the sun spoke with them; other birds spoke with them; the waters and the trees spoke with them. They all prepared for the flight together. They remembered it was time to fly, time to heed the call of nature that urged them forward. The Universal Language spoke with them in unison through all the life that came together in that instant, for the purpose of survival, expansion, and love. I witnessed the cooperation within nature, how it was so deeply interrelated and worked as a unified field. Instead of seeing the birds and trees and all elements as separate manifestations of life, I saw them as a whole, united with the pulse of this language. The language was alive, ancient and immortal. As the speakers changed, it continually evolved. The Universal language served the Great Mystery and the Creator. It served Goodness. It served the evolution of the entire cosmos.

Then I observed the greater web of life, the one I had seen from the far away quiet place. This web was also in all of life and creatures and land on Planet Earth. And it was also connected to the larger web of Cosmic life. But interestingly enough, many of the connections of these two webs, the places where the Earth web and Cosmic web met, were faint. It was as if the doors had been closed, or not used, or forgotten for quite some time. It was as if the energy flowing through the Earth web was much weaker than the energy flowing in the larger Cosmic web.

I became fascinated by this vision. Mother felt my interest, and perked up.

"The Universal language flows through and travels through these webs," She said. "I am delighted you can see and sense them. Let us go in for a closer look."

As if flying together like birds, Mother and I entered the Earth web. We followed it as if being drawn by a sacred wind. It took us to many different places all around the globe. I noticed a particular flow, a magnetic pull that kept us flying inside the "tube" more easily. As soon as we left the filament, we would not move as fast. I also noticed that many sacred sites had been built where the filaments met, not only in a criss-cross fashion, but also vertically with the cosmic web. We stopped at a place where an ancient temple had been. There were only remnants now, but I could see the horizontal and vertical lines very clearly. Had the ancient ones known this? How could they? Mother read my thoughts:

"They knew and understood the Universal Language, and used these places as a sacred portal to commune with their divine and earthly origins."

All around the world, I saw natural and man-made sacred sites built along this web. From all cultures and religions, many had interdependently built their worship areas there. I found this powerful and fascinating.

Then we travelled through great expanses of land. On many occasions the grid became heavy, disjointed, even disappeared at times. I concluded that the Earth grid was weak. Few of the sacred sites remained, and those that did were in danger of extinction by overpopulation and modernization; the cities were taking over. The spread of human beings was getting very large. The Universal Language could not travel unobstructed anymore. It was getting weak. Very weak.

Yet, I also saw the beauty of the grids that were still active. Many were in secluded places where only a few people took care of them. Some were more popular. Their power attracted many people to them. Yet many of the people had forgotten how to care for them, or did not leave offerings, or simply had forgotten the Old Ways. The grid was still alive, but it needed help. It needed to be cared for by the humans, and it also needed to be opened again to the heavens, to the Cosmic web.

Mother and I stopped again at another place. A group of people had gathered there and were proceeding with a sacred ceremony. It was high up in the mountains, and the people had walked a very long way from their villages to come and make offerings. This pilgrimage was normal for them, and it was important and essential to their culture that everyone had a chance to make it to the sacred site. The young and old were aided by the able and strong. Each took a turn to place food, sacred items, stones, and plants on a rock formation which stood at the centre of the crossing ley lines. They sang to the place and played the drums, but mostly they prayed quietly. They camped out for the night and continued the ceremony overnight. I could see the vitality in the web getting stronger as they continued with their rituals. What was so spectacular was the energy coming from the Cosmic web. It was as if an explosion of Beauty occurred where the two webs met. It was stunning.

"The places where the Earth and Cosmic grids meet are precious to me," Mother confided. "It is where I feel most alive, where I get energized. They help me connect to my divine origin and remember my purpose. When the pathways are obstructed, I cannot know myself as well. It is like being disjointed. I cannot regenerate as fast, and I cannot keep up with all the changes. I become weak."

I could see that what she was saying was true. There were many places where the light in the web did not shine as brightly. Some places were darkened even, thick and heavy. These were places in the big cities where very little natural environment was left. Interestingly, it was the individual souls that provided light to the web. I could clearly see those who were awake to their light, who had grown soul strength and stamina. They shone and were part of the grid's network. They remembered the Universal Language. They prayed. They communed. They remembered. Their remembering was in service to the whole, in service to the Earth Mother. I wondered if I could tell who these 'awakened' souls were in my earth walk, and if I had ever come across one of them before.

"Most people do not notice them," Mother informed me, "but I do. And so do the spirit beings. What is mostly invisible to the human eye does not go unnoticed in the sacred web of life. There are human beings who are Shining Ones in service to the Earth, and for them I am most grateful."

I could sense Mother Earth's love for these "shining ones", and I became mesmerized by the source of light that came from their individual souls. It was clear they were providing a similar light and vibration that existed naturally in the healthy parts of the web. Much of nature emanated that same light as well, but some of the human beings shone brighter. It was like being drawn to a small sun. I decided to take a closer look.

I was drawn to the urban expanse of New York city. I recognized the location immediately because of the Statue of Liberty. It was nighttime, and I saw a light that seemed to outshine the city lights a hundred-fold. I came closer and noticed an old man pushing a trolly of cleaning supplies. He was in a school. The desks were small, so I guessed it was an elementary school. The old man whistled joyously as he went about doing his humble work. I could see the clarity of his thoughts and the purity of his heart. He had a deep love for children and a pure desire to serve them. He was old now and did not speak English well, so he poured his love in the cleaning of this school. Nothing more, nothing less. His genuine and loving presence could be felt and seen for miles.

Then my vision took me across the ocean and land onto the high plateaus of the Himalayas. In a hidden valley where an ancient village still stood, there were caves up on the rock cliff. They were so high I wondered how anyone could ever get up there. I saw a woman, meditating and praying. Her light shone bright. She was on an inner journey. It was her way to be of service to the world. She was not fully on the Earth plane. Her emancipated body barely held weight. But on the grid, she was strong. She held the space and vibration for a portal in that region.

Then my attention came to the Amazon. The place felt familiar. I saw an intermittent light and a bright shining one. I came for a closer look, and noticed it was Joni and don Luis! How delightful it was to see them alive and well. I had almost forgotten about them. I was so enthralled by the experience with Mother Earth. Joni's light was not very strong compared to the medicine man's, yet I could see it was like a bud ready to open. They were still in ceremony.

Seeing them made me remember I had been pulled into an experience with the serpent spirit Amaru, and that was how I had come to be in the presence of Mother Earth, learning from her. As I looked onto the ceremonial scene in the Amazon, I wondered what was real. All the worlds I had visited felt far away yet intimately related. Which world was real? I was experiencing a dream within a dream within a dream. Like Alice tumbling down the rabbit hole, I had come across experiences my mind could have never imagined or made up. I looked at Joni and don Luis and wondered if I would ever find my way home again. That made me laugh. Where was home, exactly? Because being with Mother Earth was being home.

CHAPTER SIXTEEN

I learned the Universal Language flowed through a system of Earth grids. It was connected to each heart, to each living soul, and each tiny speck of life. By knowing this silent language, people found the sacred locations on Earth to make offerings and restore Beauty. I understood these grids needed to be fed by human reverence, love and heartfelt gratitude. They are important to honor, important to feed and nurture, and important to re-establish the connection with the Cosmic grid of life.

"But how can we do this, Mother, if we have forgotten the Universal Language and don't know where the grid is?" I was not sure I could see it with my physical eyes. How could the "earth Carmen" do this?

"Any place that moves you, any place that holds a special spot in your heart, any place that takes your breath away with its Beauty is also part of the grid. These are all good places to start to honor me."

When I heard these words a deep passion welled up in me, and I let my spirit soar. I wanted to travel the Earth and find the places that inspired great Beauty and awe. So I flew over many places and saw extraordinary things. Places of Beauty that were both accessible to human visitors and also so remote that only nature could witness. I saw the expanse of the Arctic region hosting a symphony of Aurora Borealis. I bounced over the vast oceans and went deep into them saying hello to the darkness and returning quickly from the bottom and catapulting into the air like a whale embracing the sky. I slithered around the floor of a rainforest like a great serpent sensing and touching the moist earth. I travelled far into the sky and saw mountain ranges that nearly touched the heavens. At the top of the highest mountain, I rested a while, sensing the presence of the Star Brothers and Sisters and the lightness of the air. I flew over to a great forest where I became a four-legged, hunting in the rich and secluded forest. I ran for miles, feeling the strength in my sleek body, the power of my flesh, the power of the sun guiding me.

Everywhere I looked, I found beauty. There was beauty above me and deep below. There was beauty every time I went to the left and to the right. There was beauty on my path before me, and all I left behind was beauty. And I knew beyond any doubt that the beauty I had experienced and seen was also within me. There was no separation from the entire body of Nature - all that existed without also existed within me. We were the same body. We were the same mind. We were united in the bosom of Creation.

Then as if I had taken a long journey, I stopped at a particular place that I had been drawn to effortlessly, as if floating in a dream. A veil opened, and I saw a large mountain surrounded by ocean. No other land could be seen. It shone like a jewel in the middle of a vast expanse of water. It was so large that I wondered how I had never heard of it before and how it could go undetected by our sophisticated satellite and GPS systems. I came closer and saw that four great rivers flowed from the top of the mountain, fed by the ever-present snow. These four rivers tumbled down the mountain all the way to the sea, nourishing life on their path.

I went near the top of the mountain where a small lake lay. Beside the lake was a large flat stone. It was made of a shining substance I was not familiar with. The entire place seemed like a cross between Earth and Sky, between Life and Death. It was no-place, no-where, but very alive. What was this place I wondered? It felt like a famed mountain, the one they speak of in the mystical texts. The Axis Mundi, the Eternal Mountain, the mountain at the centre of the world. Its sacredness was evident.

I sensed Mother Earth's presence. Her voice spoke in my heart.

"Continue," she said. "This is important. I want you to know this part of your origin. It is who you are. It is the journey. It is your soul."

I felt awkward. I wasn't sure what to do. One moment I was taking a spirit flight all over the beautiful Earth feeling ecstatic and free, and the next I was in this odd etherial place. I sat on the flat rock and waited. Before me was the small lake. It looked like a still, crystal clear mirror. There was no wind and barely a movement in the air, which struck me as strange at the top of a mountain. But this was no ordinary place.

Night came and the stars shone brightly. There was a glowing effervescent hue everywhere; in the water, the rocks, the vegetation, and even the surrounding air. Nothing stirred for a long time. So I sat still, being with the mountain, sensing its presence within me, becoming one with it like I had learned to do with Mother Earth. I was not yet sure what she wanted me to learn here, why I had been guided to this place. So I waited and communed and became even more still.

Suddenly, a cool wind stirred. I remained in stillness, listening. My eyes were closed, and yet I knew I was not alone. I felt a presence behind me. I was not sure what to do. A gentle voice instructed me to look up into the night sky. And as I did, where there had been stars above me, now it looked like a whirlpool. There was a window, an opening in the sky. And from the opening, in a swirling spiralling motion on a wave of rainbow light came a being. It looked like a hummingbird, and I was shocked to see how such a little being could fly so high up this mountain and descend from a place way above. But it did not seem phased out at all. The little hummingbird flew down the spiral as if surfing a giant cosmic wave. I was impressed. It came and landed beside me. I looked behind me and was surprised a fire had been built. And by the fire stood a radiant being of light.

"Come closer," the being told me. As I got closer, I noticed the fire was not an ordinary fire. It did not use wood and looked like it was burning on its own. "This is the fire of consciousness," the being answered. "It burns your thoughts. It burns what you think is real. It will let you know where you are on your path of life. It will burn away what is no longer serving you." I reflected on this, wondering how this was done. And the answer came: "Simply look into the flame and let your mind be open and free."

I did as the being asked. I became still and let myself be mesmerized by the fire. It wasn't too difficult. Fire always had a hypnotic effect on me. Grandmother would sing me songs, and I would often find my spirit dancing with the fire. Just as I recalled that memory, I found myself dancing with this fire. The motion of the dance took me into and through the hole in the sky, swirling up and up far into space. And there, I saw many galaxies, suns being born and some dying. In this place, I saw the beginning of all life and many, many endings. From this place, I looked down and saw the opening in the sky that led to the mountain. I saw this mountain existed on Earth but on a different plane of existence. I was stunned to see them both co-exist. The Shangri-La that mystics have spoken of truly did exist, and I wondered why it was being shown to me. Then I saw humanity spiralling around the sacred mountain. At the apex was our greatest potential in human form, and there were few beings there. The strand of human lives looked like an endless necklace of pearls going up in spiral-like fashion. But there was no up or down, only an evolution towards consciousness, towards wholeness. And as some moved up the mountain and reached the top, they would dissolve into the space above and be reborn again at the bottom of the mountain.

"The first shall be last, and the last shall be first," the being said. "There is no difference. What matters is the mountain itself, the essence and beauty of it, and what it represents. It is the soul of humanity."

I was speechless. Humanity had a soul. So far I had learned about the individual soul and also that Mother Earth had a soul. But the thought that humanity had a soul was truly revolutionary for me.

"And for the soul of humanity to grow, for it to fulfill its divine purpose, it must follow the laws given to it. These laws are to be found on and in this mountain. The original people of the Earth knew these laws and practiced them. Those were times before language as you know it. In those days, most used telepathic communication. Matter was not so dense. This is why most do not see this place and most have not found their way to it. You will return one day, one day written on the winds of time. But first, it suffices for you to know about the soul of humanity. Every pearl in the strand has meaning, has a purpose. Some still live on this mountain, but many have forgotten. So go back into your world and learn and practice the Laws. That way, the density that the soul of humanity has accumulated will start to lift, and many will find their way home again."

And at that, the being dissolved. I could not see it any more, yet its presence left a fragrance in the air. I was left alone on the top of this mountain. I tried to go down to explore, but I was only permitted to stay near the top. "Another time," the now familiar voice said to me. So I sat on the flat stone and looked into the still pool of water that lay before me. It shimmered with the light of the stars. Everything stood still as if the Earth had stopped spinning. I started to drift from the place where I sat, and the next thing I knew, I was once again in the presence of Mother Earth. The mountain had completely dissolved into thin air, just like the being had.

"What was that all about, Mother?" I asked inquisitively.

"I wanted you to know of the origin of Beauty, dear Carmen, and of the existence of the soul of humanity. This sacred mountain is within me as well. I have been tasked to look over the soul of humanity. And now, you know more about it."

I wasn't sure why this was so important to know. Why would it matter that the soul of humanity was alive? The strand of lights looked similar to the ones I had seen in the web of life. Yet it was different - humanity on its own had a different destiny than life. I gasped at my own thinking, at this revelation.

"There is no way of knowing if humanity will remain as part of the inhabitants of my body. It is said that those who remember the Old Ways, their origins, will build a new world. And after some time, those who choose to continue to live outside the universal laws of life will not be able to remain on Earth. Harmony and wholeness is an essential purpose of life. The heavy burdens created from living out of harmony with the Laws will not be tolerated indefinitely. One day, all will change."

Mother became very quiet. I was stunned by these statements. What was even more interesting was her reaction - although she cared for all her children, part of humanity's destiny was out of her hands, and she knew it.

So if the destiny of humanity was out of the hands of Mother Earth, then in whose hands was it? How much choice does humanity have in the matter? What greater purpose was humanity created for? These were not ordinary questions. And these were questions I had never asked myself before. I was too busy living my life according to the rules of my culture and society. But what if there were other rules to the game, rules that were written in our very fabric, rules that we were made to abide by, respect, and honor? Just like the law of gravity holds a reality in place, are there rules for the soul of humanity?

"The world is never what you perceive it to be," chimed Mother. Her voice was gentle, like a mother reassuring her child. "I have taken you on a journey across creation. You have witnessed the birth of galaxies and the death of suns. You have witnessed my birth and the birth of our beloved sun, without which none of life could exist on this unique and beloved planet. It took billions of years to create the right environment that could host life. Life as you know it is but a glimpse in the evolution of life. The current environment will change. I know this. I have witnessed countless births and deaths. Even I will wither away one day. And even the sun will die. None of our beloved solar system will exist as we know it. All of life in the universe is bound to a divine cycle. Some are very short, and some last millions, billions and trillions of years. But eventually all will die."

If I could get a stiff drink in this place, this would be a good time for it. Mother continued, "But without death, no life could exist. The particles that form any living body are within you as well. When a star explodes, all its particles are scattered, and these are the very building blocks that form you, and me, and all life in the universe. Death serves life. In the decay what was transforms into what can be. It took many years to develop into what we know to be the present moment. Your ancestors have sacrificed themselves for you, just as your body will return to the earth to serve the coming new life and generations. Mine too will die one day. I am prepared for this. And all is well."

Are you kidding me? Mother was mentioning this in such a nonchalant way, it made me shudder. But what was the point of living so we could die? Something hit me. If human beings knew instinctively about death, that all things die, how easy would it be to believe that they needed to honor each living moment? I tried to rationalize. There were essentially two camps of people, one would use this knowledge from fear and hoard what they could because what did it matter anyway. The other camp would use the same instinct to continue bringing forth the same delicate balance that brought them life. They would treat life with reverence, respect, and sacred reciprocity.

"The key lies in living in the present moment," Mother explained.

I had heard this many times before but did not grok its true meaning.

"You've forgotten one very important thing, dear Carmen: life serves the growth and evolution of the soul. And the soul is eternal. And it has one great purpose - to return to its Source."

Woah! That was intense. I wasn't sure how to wrap my mind around that one. Something inside me knew that I wouldn't get my answer through my normal rational channels. So I let my mind expand, wanting to be introduced to the present moment. I waited for the introduction and was met with total darkness. Then it dawned on me; I had been focusing on Creation, on Life. But in between there was so much space. I let my mind and all that I knew dissolve into that space. It felt like a giant cloud, one where all the years of evolution did not exist anymore. It consumed me, it took me apart, it took me into a deep state of un-knowing. In this place, I could not engage in any thought. Nothing existed except for my breath and my connection to life. The spark of life shone within me like the brightest jewel I had ever seen. This tiny spark held the power of creation within it. I realized this spark was in any life form throughout the universe. I could choose to visit countless life forms, and I knew the spark within each of them would be the same. There was no difference. What was highly personal became deeply impersonal. I could go anywhere, a light in a budding galaxy, a stone in Africa, part of the galactic sun, a cockroach, even a cancer cell. What I knew as "I" became "I AM." Then I dissolved into the un-knowing again.

I understood in that moment that the evolution of the Universal Soul in its myriad forms danced with the light of creation. They co-existed, serving one another, and were together as divine partners. Then I heard a cosmic laugh. It came from the heart and belly of the Divine Creator and Creatrix. And for a moment, a precious moment like a skip between time and space or a heartbeat, all of the Universe re-membered itself.

I dropped down from this experience like a down feather floating in the air and descending to the ground. I found myself gently nestled in the energy field of Mother Earth. Slowly, I came to a more conscious awareness.

"You have discovered the power of your Soul, dear Carmen. You have tasted your origin. You have a sense that what you hold on to so tightly as "you" is merely part of the Truth. You now know that you are part of the Living Universe no matter what form your life may take. You have discovered the most important part of you is immortal. The elixir of life lives within you. As you dissolved into nothingness, your truth was revealed."

CHAPTER SEVENTEEN

All was quiet. All that could be heard was the sound of Mother's heart beat and the Song of the World. The beauty of the soul of humanity revealed itself in its splendor. Intertwined with this soul was the soul of Mother Earth. Many things were similar, but they had a distinct difference. We were dependent on the Earth for our survival and evolution - yet she was not dependent on us. I had to take a deep breath after this revelation and repeat to myself: She is not dependent on us. We are guests on this beloved planet. Only guests. And as a good host, she is gracious, very gracious. Do we treat her the same? Are we good guests on this planet?

I took one look at the current state of humanity and I knew the answer to that question. Guests respect their hosts. They do not take more than what is needed. And if they mean to stay longer than expected, they do something to contribute to the household. I had a cousin who came over to my place once. She meant to stay a few days while she found some work. The days turned into weeks, and the weeks turned into months. I didn't notice too much because I was working so hard. One day, she had a friend move in without telling me. The place was a disaster. She ate my food and rarely replaced what she took. And she was ungrateful. She felt it was my duty to help her because I had so much more than she did. She took and took until I had to change the locks on her. I almost had to call the police a few times, but finally her ego took the better of her, and she stopped bothering me. I never knew what happened to her.

She never spoke to me again. I heard rumours she had moved to New Brunswick, but I never found out for sure.

I thought of my cousin while looking at humanity. How different are we on this planet? Do we offer our help, gifts, and clean up after ourselves? Or do we act like our species is the most important one of all and remove what comes in the way of quenching our ever-growing desires?

And with these thoughts, nightmarish scenes unfolded before me. I saw the destruction mankind was capable of. Everything from cruelty toward its own children, to the devastation of the forests, and the pollution of the waters. It was like watching a gut-wrenching horror movie, and there was nothing I could do about it. I tried to intervene, to reverse the cutting of the forests, stop a murder, and the severe beating of a child from taking place, but I could not. I was in a frenzy. I called upon Mother Earth to stop it. I screamed to the heavens demanding to know why Creator and Creatrix would allow this to happen. I felt the pain, the suffering, the grief, the loss, the fear of the countless beings that died in the name of progress, of the illness that humanity carried within it. Most of all, I was ashamed. I was ashamed to be part of this insanity, that it was my species causing so much suffering to itself, the planet, and all other living creatures. The intensity was too much to bear. It felt like I was in a living hell. It took all my strength to break free from the visions. Finally, I was catapulted into the air, hovering once again in the familiar territory that Mother Earth and I shared. Mother gave me the time and space to regain my composure. What I experienced was horrible. How could a living hell exist like that? Where was higher justice? I did not understand. I felt betrayed and responsible for the insanity at the same time. What a contrast it was to experience this as opposed to the blissful beauty of moments before. I never wanted to experience the intense suffering again. Was that why so little was being done to stop it? Because the pain was so great? Was it easier to ignore than to feel, and simpler to stick our heads in the sand? I was more confused than ever.

Mother's soft voice broke my thought pattern, and I was grateful.

"Little One, remember you have a choice. You always have a choice. And don't worry so much - look."

We travelled a little further into space until planet Earth was barely recognizable. She looked beautiful with the backdrop of the solar system and other stars. I was grateful to be further away from the aura of humanity. And I realized that the sphere of influence of humanity was actually quite small. And somehow I found it comforting to know that we are only hurting ourselves. But why take down the innocent with our ignorance even if it only belonged on Earth? Something really did not feel right about that. Not right one bit. And I got very angry. What gave us the right to treat life that way? Thank goodness the insanity was contained to our planet, and the rest of the universe was safe. But still, the focus was on this planet, my planet. And this was my species. It was my responsibility to do my best to turn things around.

From what I gathered from Mother Earth's teachings, it was clear that no other species on Earth had the power, desire or need to control the environment to provide for its desires. No other species was stupid enough to alter the face of the Earth to suit their own needs alone. Perhaps there were other places in the universe that carried life, and perhaps they too had made the mistakes we were making. If only they were here to tell. I sensed Mother wanted to answer this question, but I was not ready to hear her answer. She backed off, and I knew she was amused, letting me grumble.

I finally calmed down. To experience and witness the destructive and chaotic nature of humanity was a lot to bear. On

Earth, living my daily life, it was so easy to ignore while I focused on my personal life and goals. Most of the time I was oblivious of the needs of those around me, unless they had something I wanted or needed. Also, I was minding my own business and certainly was not fighting a war or killing people or abusing children. I was living a small selfish life. No matter how successful I had become, I had lost everything because it was built on greed and a shallow acceptance of life. My life had no real meaning, no depth, nothing I could set forth with pride and love for the generations to come.

As I reflected on what was shown to me, I became appalled at the lack of action from humanity that would and could stop the nonsense. What made us so numb and complacent? And I remembered Mother showing me the web of life - we had forgotten the universal language and were no longer in touch with all our relations. We had forgotten about sacred relationship. I knew that humanity had the potential to live in harmony with nature, with life, with one another. To do so was in fact our true purpose, our highest potential and our responsibility. It was written in the soul of humanity, and I had experienced it. Right action was essential at this juncture in time. But what could I do? How could I begin the healing journey towards wholeness and play my part in the healing of the planet?

Mother knew what to say, "Learn to establish a relationship of trust between you and the natural world. So much of that trust has been lost. And like a broken heart, it needs mending. Do not force the relationship. Let it happen naturally. No relationship can be forced by willing yourself on another. Relationships are built on a foundation of trust. They are nourished by love. They are sustained day by day. Never take for granted a relationship in your life as each bond is a living grace and a choice by each participant. To be in relationship is to participate in the Great Game of life. So to heal, start by healing yourself. Heal your relationship with your soul, re-member who and what you are, and what the meaning of your life is. Then, once your authentic nature is shining forth, you can begin to develop sacred relationships in your life.

She paused for a bit, then continued, "Take our relationship for example. Why do you believe we have met? Why have we come together in this way?" Now that's a million dollar question, I thought. But I knew Mother would not let me off the hook. So I quieted my mind and contemplated her question. Images of the past few days appeared before me in a similar fashion as my life review. At first I saw myself in the present moment, hovering in some kind of inter-space with Mother. I was not sure where I was. It could have been in the cave where Amaru took me, but it felt like an adjacent realm above Earth, connected to both earth reality and sky/cosmic reality. I had not bothered to find out specifically where I was while experiencing this journey with Mother Earth. Yet now, it seemed like an important point to know and understand. It was as if we were in a massive information library. For some strange reason, this made sense to me. How else would have I accessed all the information from the visions so clearly and effortlessly? When I focused on this place, everything became bright and clear. All the information from the individual souls, the soul of humanity, and of nature were recorded in this place. It was like a super computer that would make Steve Jobs drool. Perhaps this was where he got the idea for the iCloud? But I digress again. Maybe this was exactly how my mind could understand and relate to the experience at hand, so I trusted my vision. The web of life was like the internet. I felt like I was in a science fiction full feature film. But the lesson was clear - all information was recorded and not a heart beat was lost in the universal library.

So, I thought. Humanity was a lot more aware of the current planetary dilemma than I anticipated. And we were so connected, more connected than ever. Had we substituted the web of life for an electronic one? What was the difference?

I answered my own questions: Love was the difference. Reverence was the difference. Deep gratitude and harmony were the difference. I saw two worlds, two systems colliding, causing friction. They mirrored one another in their likeness, but one was only a poor substitute for the other. What would happen if these two systems merged? If technology was grounded in the Earth grid and they were in sacred partnership?

Then something extraordinary happened; the planet came alive with such force that I thought I was looking at the sun for a moment. It was as if a burst of light came from the very core of the earth, expanding outward in rays that almost reached the moon. And for a few precious moments the entire planet shone this way. Mother Earth was shining in all her Glory. Life and Light co-existed in perfect relationship. And I heard the familiar cosmic laughter again, the one that brought clear memory of Creator and Creatrix.

I was stunned by this vision. Yet again my perception was blown into pieces. Was there truly a power that can change the course of human destiny in one single moment?

What this vision was showing me was the potential of humanity. And the fact that we were not in control, not any where near it. It was possible, in the blink of an eye, that a force much greater than humanity and life could restore the health of the planet. But it made me wonder; what I perceived as a moment could be many thousands of years or just a few decades. But it was possible. It was possible for humankind to live in harmony once again. And it was also possible for humanity to wipe itself out off our beloved little blue dot, and I knew the planet would recover very nicely.

I wondered what was the link to technology and the fact the world had become so much smaller. It seemed it was a way for us to stay connected to life, to one another. Yet what passed through the currents was filled with all emotions and thoughts that belonged to humanity. There was beauty and deep ugliness. There was peace and chaos.

It was possible to "wake-up" to a new reality, just as I had witnessed in the glow of the planet. What mattered was that Mother Earth desired growth. She remembered her origin and her purpose. She knew she was made of star dust, just like us, and she knew she was the host to a multitude of living creatures who were born, lived, and died in the Great Game of Life.

Because it was a game, wasn't it? In the big picture, we would decide our fate. Would it be our destiny to succumb to fear, or would we rise to meet the transforming qualities of love? Would we continue in our suffering, or would we brave the pain of life with dignity and be courageous enough to live a good life? I let my thoughts consider all options. And after a while, I became detached from the outcome.

"Good, Carmen. Now you are beginning to understand. Humanity's fate is not in my hands, or yours, or in the hands of life. Many species have gone extinct, and every one is subject to the universal laws of change. No one is exempt. So if we know we will die and transform one day, what matters most is what we do with the life that has been entrusted to us. I too live by these rules. And together, we will learn. And together, we will grow."

I became very tired. This was a lot of information to absorb, and my ability to digest was exhausted. I had enough information now. I knew I had received what I needed to learn.

"I hope I can remember what you have so graciously shared with me, Mother. I am afraid this was only a dream, and when I wake up, I won't remember any of it," I was sad yet hopeful.

"You will find a way, dear Carmen. The past is the future, and the future is past. You will find your way back to your remembrance of who you are, and when you do, I will be there to welcome you home, child."

The tiredness came over me. I drifted into a deep slumber and felt I could be unconscious for years. I wanted to rest, to rest for a very long time. In the distance, I heard a heart beat, a familiar rhythm. I travelled toward its nourishing sound. The deeper I went into rest the louder it got. I was resting at the bosom of the Mother, nestled in her loving embrace.

"Remember Me," a gentle voice chimed in with the heart beat. "Remember Me." And I drifted into unconsciousness.

CHAPTER EIGHTEEN

All I could hear was the sound of a pounding heart. It was faint at first, but it became so loud that it jolted me out of my slumber and into consciousness. I was back in the large cave at the centre of the earth, lying on the ground by the fire. I was disoriented at first, trying to remember where I was and where I had been. Slowly the memories of my journey and the lessons with Mother Earth came back. I liked being close to the fire in this cave because it reminded me of Her. I realized that my energy field was not merged with hers anymore, and I felt a vast emptiness. I longed for her presence. I knew the experience was over. A part of me wanted to know more, to be with her again and for a longer time. But I knew I had been given a great gift and was grateful for it. I bowed to the fire and thanked Mother for her blessings and all she had taught me. Out of the corner of my eye, I saw a movement at the entrance of the cave. Amaru stirred from her sleep. She uncoiled her massive, sleek body and came near.

"Ah! You have returned!" She hissed lovingly. "Did you receive the medicine you needed?"

I didn't need to think that through, "Yes, Amaru, I did."

"Good. Let's return," she responded in a keen way. "I'm famished."

I wasn't sure if I should be worried about becoming a meal. Then I remembered I was in my spirit form. She could go ahead and eat me if she wanted, but I knew that was not my destiny. And I did not fear death anymore. In fact, I feared life a great deal more.

She instructed me to follow her out of the cave. My consciousness was part of hers, similar to when I had merged with Mother Earth. I felt her long body hugging and touching the moist earth. No wonder she was such a trusted ally and guardian of Mother Earth - she knew her intimately; she kept so close to her skin. I could even sense the pulse of the Earth, the one that came from the centre core. It was pounding in unison with the great serpent's movements.

We emerged from the tunnel just as the first morning light of the sun touched the land. It had rained, and the ray of light made the green so vibrant, even the eyes of my spirit needed to adjust. The beauty of the forest took my breath away. I had never seen it this way, so alive, so diverse, so connected. I knew without a doubt that all the living creatures, the elements, the rocks, everything, were connected. What I had experienced and seen as the web of life with Mother Earth was now so fully alive I was experiencing it a thousand fold because I was so close to it.

Amaru's spirit started to detach from mine. But before she went on her way, she said, "Remember me. Remember the power of my medicine. Each time you long for connection and for the warmth of Mother Earth, enter the darkness and look for me. I will be waiting in the deepest caverns of your mind, in the crevices of your heart, in the imprints of your soul, and I will guide you to what you need most. I have the gift of life and transformation. Many have feared me, but not you, not anymore. You and I are allies now. Call on me, and I will come. You know how to find me." And at that she disappeared in the thick underbrush of the forest, surely to find her next meal.

I was bewildered. The detachment from Mother Earth, and now from Amaru, had left me feeling empty. But not really, I realized. Their presence was gone, yes, but now I felt the forest even more. Dog came by and found me as if he had been waiting for me all along. He was filled with joy to see me. How he was attuned to this I was not sure, but I welcomed him wholeheartedly. I stayed near the entrance of the tunnel for a while, being with dog and the forest, taking my time to adjust to my new senses.

After some time, I returned slowly toward the village. Dog seemed to know the way and lead me slowly through the jungle. The sun had risen much higher in the sky by the time I reached the village. It was abnormally quiet. The ceremonial fire had gone to ashes, and many were in their huts and had gone to sleep. Some of the old ones were watching the young and slowly tidying up from the previous evening. Joni was fast asleep in her hut, and even don Luis was taking a nap. I remembered about the Ayahuasca ceremony and concluded the participants had likely been up all night. I hoped I would be able to share my experiences with Joni one day and was curious to hear about her experience too.

I had not been around these people very long, as a matter of fact I had never actually met them in physical form, and what I knew of them came from my observations. But it felt like I knew them intimately. Their movements, habits, expressions, and tendencies were familiar. Their way of life made sense to me, and I tasted the simplicity of their life pace and the richness of their soul. I could see much more now, after spending some time with Mother Earth. What I believed to be primitive before now held a depth of meaning, especially the rituals and celebrations. My journey to the centre of the Earth, to the heart and soul of Mother Earth, had changed my perception drastically. I knew I had changed. I knew something had transformed in me. My world would never be the same again. It was as if a veil had been lifted, and my neurosis with it.

I continued to explore the village and felt a wave of compassion come over me. I loved these people, and I loved Joni. I loved the synchronicities that had brought me to this exact place at this exact time. I felt immersed in the web of life and finally found my place within it. It felt like home.

Finally, I could not resist anymore and went towards my body. I felt immense compassion for it. She and I had travelled this earth journey together, and I had forgotten how precious my body was. I treated it more like a commodity and a fast car, needing it to be perfect, and believed most of the time it was a nuisance. As I saw her lying there helpless, I was deeply moved by my body's innocence. I knew it was the kindness of Joni, don Luis, the boy apprentice and the goodness of the people that kept me alive. But it wasn't only them; the forest, nature, Mother, and my spirit allies were all contributing to my vitality and survival. All of them watched over me in a way I had never ever looked after or cared for anyone before. I had an IV that was keeping me hydrated and alive that was true, yet what was truly feeding me was their love, tenderness and respect. I wondered if I would ever wake up. I wondered where my story would end. I wondered if I deserved to live again.

I had no idea how much time had passed. So much had happened, yet it did not seem that many days had passed on Earth. I wondered how long could a person remain in a coma like that? I decided to remain close to my body. I felt drawn to it and had a desire to remain close and protect it. I did not want to miss anything. I spoke to it and prayed for it. It was odd, as if I was releasing, forgiving, and letting go of all my past. All that I had been shown by my guide Angie in my life review, all that I did not adhere to anymore, I wanted to heal. So I stuck nearby. Dog was close too, yet he was very timid and rarely showed himself to humans. But at night, when he could be less detectable and my body was alone in the healing lodge, he would come near and sit by my side, and we would both watch over my body together. He was a delightful companion. Somehow we understood one another. When times were particularly tough for me, he would diligently stay by my side.

I was beginning to have a better sense of day and night simply because I made an effort to pay attention to it.

I was curious to see if my body emitted a soul light and if it was connected to the grid. I noticed that my body had a faint glow to it but did not have much soul strength. Perhaps this was because part of me was hovering in spirit form outside of it. I did not know. The glow emanating from it was akin to the glow I noticed around stones and rocks. Pulsing slowly, but deeply, and not emitting many spurts of life or shining too brightly. Perhaps this was akin to being in a coma. I looked for the web of life around me and noticed don Luis instantly. It was interesting how I was able to "tune-in" at will to the web of life. It was as if when I thought of the web and desired to see it, it would simply show up. The medicine man's light was profound and so were many of the souls in the village. And the web of life formed a cluster around the centre village, where the ceremonies took place. It was like a node made of filaments of light. Nature and the environment were connected as well. And it was as if the people lived in symbiotic relationship with the environment around them. The filaments of light were actually visible to me. My inner sight had awakened, free of the distractions of my senses. This was how I learned to "see".

My vision took me back to my body, and as I looked deeper, I could see I was not connected to the web of life. I was shocked and saddened by this, yet was not surprised. I somehow knew that I had lost this connection many moons ago. As soon as I thought that, I was taken back to my childhood at a particularly loving moment with grandmother. She was showing me how to pick a tree for canoe making. "Before we head to the forest," she said, "we must call to the tree spirits to aid us. Today we will take the life of one of their brothers, and we must be clear in our intent, pure in our hearts, and always ask Great Spirit for guidance and permission." She picked up her drum and sang a beautiful song. Once she was done, she took an offering of tobacco and reverently placed it in a small bowl. She prayed deeply over it, and when she was complete, she lit the tobacco in the bowl. She blew her prayers to Great Spirit. "Always reveal yourself before you take a life, child. Always ask for permission. Taking a life is a grace, not a right. Remember this." Her serious demeanor changed instantly. "Now! Let's go see how nature has responded!" She had the excitement of a child. She picked up her bag and put some fresh bannock in it with a little jar of honey and some water. "Come, Carmen, let's go find our tree." As we walked out from her cabin into the forest, I could clearly see her soul light and how connected she was to the web of life. And so was I. And I was happy.

So, I thought, I was not always disconnected. There was a time in my life when I was close to life, part of it. How in the world did I shut it out? And more importantly, why would I even want to? I sat near my body contemplating this. Then don Luis came into the Healing Lodge. He looked at me with a look that meant "pay attention". I had almost forgotten he could see me. He took his rattle and started to shake it rhythmically all over my body. He was chanting. He stopped over my abdomen and started to rattle intensely over my liver. As he did this, I literally saw a darkness like fumes coming out of it, almost like black smoke. As the smoke freed itself from by body, my mind connected to it. And I immediately thought of a fight I'd had with my mother. It was when she decided not to let me see my grandmother anymore. I was devastated. I screamed. I yelled. I called her names. I told her I hated her. She told me that my grandmother was poisoning me with her ways and she would not tolerate it any longer. She did not like what had happened to "her people" and was convinced that staying away from them was the solution. I was so devastated by this that I hid in the closet for three days. I refused to come out. My grief was too much to bear. As it turned out my father would sneak me away to see grandmother anyway. But something never felt right after this fight with mother. She made me feel like I was an imposter in my own family and did not deserve grandmother's love. I had never forgiven her.

As the smoke left my body, I remembered all this. And it felt terrible. Don Luis looked at me again and asked me to follow his actions. I saw him call in healing grace and with a large feather he fanned the smoke away. As he did this, small bubbles of vibrating light came close to my body and merged with it where the black density had been. And my body shone a little brighter!

I understood in that moment that the experience with my mother many years ago had still been living inside me, creating an obstacle to being connected with the web of life. I understood that I must clear these experiences from my body, mind and heart. I understood if I did this, my body would have a chance to connect to the web again, and perhaps, perhaps she would wake up. This possibility filled me with hope.

So over the next three days, I purged. It was a horrible experience. I worked alongside the medicine man. Each time he did a ritual over my body, I would go through a major release of emotional and psychological pain. Each one of my major life choices were revisited. It was excruciating. Joni sat by my side, and I heard her tell me stories. Her voice kept me going; it was the link to my body and a chance to live again. I felt I was lost in a realm of hell, purging and releasing. These were the darkest days of my life. I did not know so much suffering was possible. Amaru was with me, consoling me, saying all was well. I did not remember the specific conversations with Mother Earth, and I longed for the freedom that I'd had in spirit form. Now that I was closer to my body, I almost regretted the desire to live. The pain was more than I could bear. How could my soul be on fire and my body lie so still? Only the shaman and Amaru knew of my predicament. On the outside everything looked still. But inward, I was in the fire of transformation. Wasn't there another way to life? Did this have to be the passage back for me?

During the life review, I was looking at my life from an objective point. I felt the impact of my decisions, but I did not live or become them. Here in this place I was reliving traumas I had endured all my life. They had become an imprint, part of my psyche so deep I did not know what was authentic and true and what was illusion. I had a fire so large burning within my soul I could have set the Amazon aflame. Don Luis kept smudging me with herbs, and the demons within fought every scent, every prayer, every thought of light, every ounce of love. But I kept at it. I could have given up anytime, but I fought hard. I don't know what made me fight so hard for life, what made me want to release the illusions and suffering. Perhaps it was my time with Mother Earth, or Joni's kindness, or the power that my grandmother transmitted to me by her unconditional love - but I held on.

Dog never left my side. Even don Luis was surprised for Dog had never come to him as an ally before. No one bothered him. They let him be. Everyone kept on playing their part. For three days and three nights I was in a living hell. Faces of loved ones, those I hated, my mother, my father, Larry, all became part of my living nightmare. I relived every ounce of pain I had inflicted on others. I lived it from their point of view. I did not know how long I could handle this. The doorway was always shown to me, the one where grandmother and the Shining Ones had met me. It was always clear that I could choose death, and I was not afraid anymore. Many times I thought dying would be so much easier than living. I did not understand the purging that was happening. But something within me was alight, and I knew it was my destiny to push on into life - even if it felt like death. In a way I knew I was choosing death, the path of death that leads to a rebirth, to an authentic life. Every part of my old self was dying, burning away, being dissolved. The shaman's herbs were purifying me. The drumming kept my heart pounding. Mother Earth was sustaining me and whispering in my soul to keep going. Just when I thought I could not take it anymore, everything went dark. The pain dissipated completely, and I was free.

CHAPTER NINETEEN

I could hear the sound of birds. There were so many of them, and they were so loud. It was as if they were singing a symphony in my mind. My head felt heavy, my body even heavier. I was warm. Where was I? I tried to open my eyes and found my eyelids almost glued shut. With strain I managed to open them a little, and it was pitch black. Had I gone blind? I tried to speak but could not. My mouth was so dry. I moved my jaw, trying to activate the muscles. It felt like they had not been used in days. I managed to open my lips and let out a croaky moan. All was quiet around me. Another attempt was a bit more successful. "Hello?" There was no response. I listened to the birds and finally made out the sound of human voices. There were children at play and people speaking, but I could not understand what they were saying. I took some deep breaths. The air was heavy and humid. And just as I was wiggling my feet and hands and finding movement there, I heard a familiar voice; it was Joni. She had been fetched by the boy, who had heard my stirrings. She entered the room at high speed.

"Carm?" she asked cautiously. "Carm are you awake?"

"Yes," I croaked.

"Oh, Carm!" she exclaimed while bursting into a flood of tears. I could tell she wasn't sure whether to hug me or punch me. She decided to kiss my forehead and hold my hand instead. I could feel her tears on my skin.

"You gave me such a fright! I am so glad you're awake," she was still crying. I waited a little for her to compose herself. I looked around and could barely see anything. I asked Joni tentatively, "Why is it so dark? Where am I?"

Joni perked up a little. "You are in the Amazon, in a small village. There are curtains around your bed to keep the light out. It is early morning, and the sun is just rising. It is November 21," Joni mentioned the last sentence slowly and inquisitively, as if looking for my reaction. "Do you remember anything?"

I paused to think. It was as if my brain had gone to sleep. I could barely recall anything. I shook my head, then I nodded, then I shook my head again. "No, I mean a little, but no," I was confused. My memory recall seemed to have shut down. At least I remembered Joni, I thought.

Joni took a deep breath. I could tell she was doing her best to see how to break some news to me. I braced myself for her answer.

"Carm, you've been in a coma for the last 10 days." My expression did not need to be translated, "What? How on earth?"

"You were bitten by a snake. The poison nearly killed you. In fact, we thought it had. If it weren't for the medicine man administering some remedies and keeping you in the coma, you would have surely died." She paused to let this information sink in. I tried to remember more but couldn't. "Transporting you to a hospital could have been deadly. I had to make a choice, Carm - to take you to a hospital, which was hours away, or to keep you closer and trust the healing experience and power of the local medicine man. Either choice was risky. And I chose to keep you near. Oh, Carmen! I hope you forgive me! I did not leave your side. I am so happy you are alive! I thought I had lost you," she started sobbing again. While Joni was composing herself, I started to remember bits and pieces. The betrayal by Larry. The trip to Peru. Flying to the Amazon. Going for a walk with Joni. Then...

"Joni! I am alive!" I exclaimed nearly jumping out of bed. Joni instinctively guided my body back down. "Yes you are, Carm. It's a miracle. We were not sure what antivenom to give you. No one saw the snake. If it weren't for don Luis showing up when he did, I don't..." She didn't want to complete her sentence, but I knew what she was referring to. She started sobbing again. This time I knew they were tears of relief, "I have not left your side for 10 days. I did everything I could to help. I promise."

I squeezed Joni's hand. "I know you did, Joni. I can't imagine any better nurse and friend to have by my side. You saved my life." I was the one crying now.

At that moment, the boy came in the darkened hut, accompanied by a man. The second I saw him, I had a sense that I knew him. I felt deeply calm. He uttered a few words in Spanish to Joni, which she translated, "He is happy you found your way back and welcomes you to his home and village." I stared at him with big eyes. The man looked amused. He uttered a few more words to Joni. "He says not to worry. He will teach you to remember. But first, you must get your strength back."

Don Luis uttered a lot of words very fast to the boy and more slowly to Joni. He seemed to be giving some directions. He and the boy left the room, and Joni was left to tend to me.

"I will take your vitals, sweetie," she cooed. Truly, I could not have been with a better person at the moment.

"And we will keep the IV on for a bit yet, until you are strong enough to drink and eat on your own. Your body still needs to purge the poison, so we want to go slowly. Don Luis is preparing medicine for you. It will make you strong, he says. And when you get your vitality back, you will remember, he says. He will take you on a journey to remember. Do you know what he is talking about?" Joni asked me as she took my blood pressure.

"I'm not sure," I replied almost stuttering. "I think I almost died. And I had strong dreams, dreams that seemed very real, more real than this world. I don't remember details, but I sense something really important happened." I knew something important had happened. I felt it. I could not express what it was, but I had changed.

"You look really peaceful and calm for someone who just came out of a coma," Joni winked at me. "And you haven't fussed about your hair once!" she teased.

I agreed. Something was different. The old Carmen would have been a basket case by now. Waking up in the deep Peruvian Amazon in a hut with a shaman and primitive medical equipment. That would have sent me through the roof. I was notorious for cleanliness and an avant-garde lifestyle, but all that felt so far away and unimportant. It was as if that part of my memory had been toned down and replaced with something more nourishing. I didn't know with what exactly, and I surely did not know how to describe it. And I wondered, was this what the don Luis was referring to? I was curious about my newfound state of peace. It was as if I had a new perspective on life. And I was keen to find out what had caused the change and how I had acquired it.

Joni filled me in on what had happened during my time in a coma. The tour had continued without us, yet the tour organizer would touch base with Felipe to get news as often as she could. We calculated the group would be in Machu Picchu by now and daydreamed about what that would be like.

Joni had arranged everything, keeping the authorities informed about our location and predicament. She had worked with a team of doctors from the nearest city and they had kept her supplied with what she needed. Felipe would travel every few days from the Lodge to bring supplies and messages. Joni had arranged that our stay in Peru would be indefinite due to medical reasons and had a contact at the Canadian Embassy in Lima. She informed them of our location and of our stay. She said they were very cooperative and would do anything they could to help. We were free to remain where we were for as long as we needed. Joni had also informed my insurance company at home, who wanted to fly me back as soon as possible to receive Canadian medical care. It took a bit of convincing, but because of Joni's expertise and qualifications, combined with the very low cost of treatment, the insurance company agreed to let me stay in Peru as long as they were taken off the hook for future liabilities. So it seemed the world had conspired to have us stay in this remote Amazonian village for a little while longer. This took a lot of pressure off.

"What about your job teaching at the hospital?" I asked Joni very concerned about her well-being. Surely she had to go back.

"Don't worry, Carm, I've already contacted them. That place was getting too stuffy anyway. Consider this a sabbatical," she beamed an exquisite smile, and I swear I could see a twinkle in her eye. Truly this was the most genuinely optimistic person I had ever met. "Let's just say I was meant to be here too. The change of pace is refreshing and exactly what I needed. Besides, I was getting out of practice from my true vocation by teaching nursing students. It's good to practice my art, and I am learning some good tricks along the way," she said as she rubbed a stinky salve on my leg. She truly was a natural healer.

My recovery took a few days. I was left in the dark for the first day, and slowly the thick straw walls were taken down to let me adjust to the light and the life of the village. Don Luis had mentioned that keeping a person in the dark was a good way not to shock the returning soul when it had been in a coma and had travelled to the inner places. Joni listened to him with an open mind. I was surprised by her acceptance of the traditional medicine and philosophy considering she had been trained in and practiced Western medicine. I knew however that her true passion lay in healing in a much broader sense of the word, and for years she had been supplementing her training with a wide range of holistic practices. So in a way, this was a natural fit for her. She spoke of don Luis with immense respect and readily learned what he taught her. It was instinctual for her to listen to his advice about leaving me in the dark and gradually introducing me to the light. "This mimics the time in the womb," he had told her. "When death comes so close to a person, one must release into its will. Whether death takes her to the other side or back to earth, the process is the same - one must always come through the womb of the Great Mother."

The stronger I got, the more light was let into the hut. At first I could barely drink the herbal concoctions, and now I was sitting up and drinking the broth myself. It was good to sit up and take in the surroundings. The children would come up and visit me now. It was a pleasure to see their radiant smiles and lovely demeanor. I smiled a lot and laughed deep belly laughs as we did our best to communicate with one another. One girl was particularly interested in my hair and kept running her hands through it.

"I've never seen you so happy and content," Joni remarked one day. She was right. The demons of my past were mysteriously gone. "You look pretty darn happy yourself," I blurted back with a smirk. She waved me off in a "its nothing" kinda way and continued with her chores.

It took a few more days to get me on my feet. When I was finally ready, I had a retinue of helpers to aid me out of the hut. I was touched by the excitement of the children. Everyone wanted a role in helping me. It felt wonderful to move my legs, stand upright, and feel the strength in my body again. Every step was like embracing the miracle of life. My feet were bare, and I could feel the warmth of the earth penetrating my legs. I breathed deeply, fully and gratefully. I paused and took a look around me. The children became more quiet, as if they knew this moment was important to me. I looked around me and saw the diversity of the life in the glorious Amazon. It was astonishing. I noticed so many details, heard sounds and smelled aromas as if I had never used my senses before. Everything was so much more vivid than I had ever experienced. It was as if I had had a reboot of my senses and a new chance at living.

One of the children came forward and offered me an odd looking fruit. I looked towards Joni to see if it was ok to eat, and she gave an encouraging nod. I wasn't sure how to eat it and looked to the girl to show me how. She picked a small piece of the exposed flesh with her fingers and took it to her lips. I proceeded to do the same, but before I could put the piece in my mouth, she insisted that she feed me hers. I let her. It was the most extraordinary fruit I had ever tasted. My expression must have shown my pleasure because she smiled with delight. She asked permission to continue feeding me, and I agreed. I could tell she was coming from a place of care and love. I was her guest and she wanted to do her part in my healing. The following moments were some of the most precious in my life. I earnestly wished the joy shared in this simple act would remain imprinted in my heart forever.

Don Luis had told Joni that he wanted to take me to a nearby sacred place as soon as I was strong enough to make the journey. For the purpose of the ritual, it was important that I walk there myself. So I kept taking longer strolls in the forest and getting stronger each time. Joni and I took many walks, and she started to teach me what she had learned about the plants and animals. There were so many new species we had never seen before. At all times we had children with us, and they took turns teaching us the words for each of the animals and the plants. On rare occasions, don Luis would join us, mostly to observe. He seemed to approve of what we were doing. Every once in a while, he would point to a plant, and his apprentice would collect it. Every time he did so, he uttered prayerful words to the plant and gave something in exchange, usually a bit of tobacco or coca leaves. He never left a hole in the earth when he took something.

The day came when we were summoned to see don Luis. He told us that we would leave in the morning, and that it was important to fast until then. He permitted us to drink water and gave us a herbal mixture to drink. Both Joni and I looked a little apprehensive, and don Luis laughed.

He told Joni, "Don't worry. It is not Grandmother Ayahuasca or any of her relatives." Joni was relieved, and she nodded to me that it was okay to drink. He would not tell her what it was, but she had learned to trust him, and I trusted her judgement.

It was before sunrise when Joni, don Luis, the boy, and I gathered by the sacred tree. Felipe showed up and wanted to join us, but don Luis would not let him come this time. He said this ritual was for the gringos and laughed out loud. So the four of us set out purposely in the cool morning air. The path was so overgrown, I wondered how don Luis found it, but he did not seem concerned. At times he and the boy had to use their machete to cut a way through the thick bush. They avoided cutting the plants as much as they could, but sometimes it was simply unavoidable. He said the place always led him there, even if the path changed. It was a sacred place protected by the spirits of the land and water. He had prepared himself for a few days before the walk and had done a ritual to commune with the spirits of the place to let them know we were coming. He had done offerings and prayers. He seemed confident that the spirits had heard him and were expecting us.

There was something special in the air. None of us spoke during the whole time. Joni and I did not dare break the silence. And although I had not eaten anything for a while, I was not hungry. The herbal mixture seemed to subdue my cravings. I had asked Joni before we left if she knew what we were going to do. She shook her head and lifted her shoulders briefly, saying she had no idea, "But let's face it. How many times in our lives will we have the opportunity to trek the rainforest with a shaman?" That seemed enough to convince her to go. As for me, I had already been bitten by a snake and almost died. I had the scar and a bit of residue swelling to prove it. What worse could happen? Granted, if it was the "old" Carmen there was no way she would have made it 10 feet out the door of the hut after the fiasco with the snake. There were way too many bugs and unknown creatures in this place. It had taken some personal convincing for me to go on that fateful walk with Joni to begin with. Now the creatures didn't phase me. They seemed like a part of me and had every right to exist in the environment. I thought that was an odd way to think. Something definitely had changed in me. I guess coming close to death changes your perspective. But was it more? I had an inkling I would find out.

Finally, after walking most of the day, we arrived at a clearing. I could hear the sound of running water, faint at first, then more like rolling thunder. As we stepped into the clearing, I saw one of the most spectacular views of my life, a stunning waterfall. To see this flowing giant in the heart of the Amazon was an ecstatic sight. The place rumbled with life. I could feel the water droplets on my skin the closer we got to it. Joni was just as impressed. She looked at me with big eyes that spoke volumes. Although we were tired, the sight and feel of this hidden treasure rejuvenated us in an instant. Don Luis' steps became faster, and he seemed pleased to have reached his destination. Joni broke the silence. Her voice sounded like a whisper against the background noise of the waterfall.

"It's amazing, isn't it? I've never seen anything like it. And it is totally off the beaten track. I don't recall having seen it in any of my guide books. You'd think they would have mentioned something like this." I agreed. It was unusual to have a sight like this kept in pristine condition and hidden from the main population and travel journals. I wondered how many places in the world were hidden from us. As I drifted off into that thought, I had an elusive feeling that I had visited such a place before, but I quickly brushed off the feeling.

Don Luis was calling us closer to him. We had reached a natural resting place with a full view of the falls. He sat down for the first time since we had set out in the early morning, and we were happy to follow suit. As soon as I sat down, I realized how hungry I was. My stomach grumbled. Don Luis handed me some water to drink and some leaves to chew on. Joni translated for me that chewing on the leaves would help take away the hunger. I was not sure if it was the fasting, the leaves, or the tangible vitality of the falls, but I felt I was coming into a slight trance state. By looking at Joni, I could tell she felt the same. Don Luis opened his medicine bundle and started to rattle and chant. The boy was quietly explaining what was happening to Joni, and Joni simultaneously explained it to me.

"He's telling the spirits of the place that we have arrived. Now he's offering gifts. That's tobacco, and chicha, and I really didn't understand what that is. Some kind of sacred root or something," Joni went on doing her best with the translation, but my mind naturally tuned out. I was getting more entranced with don Luis' ceremonial voice.

I must have zoned out because the next thing I heard was Joni's voice saying, "It's time for your Baptism."

CHAPTER TWENTY

Pardon me? My baptism? I must have really zoned out. I tried to ask Joni more questions, but she was in deep conversation and walking really close to the boy. She was totally enthralled. So I quietly followed.

Don Luis led us down a path. We were at the top of a ridge and needed to get down closer to the falls. As soon as we started our descent, it began to rain. And I am not talking ordinary rain - it was torrential. We were in the rainforest after all. I was surprised it hadn't rained so far on this journey. The shaman mentioned it was a good omen, that the spirits had heard us. I had to focus really hard not to slip. We were completely drenched in no time. It didn't seem to phase the Peruvians one bit. After some skillful maneuvering, we finally reached our destination.

At the bottom of the waterfall was a clear pool of water. This was unusual as most of the water sources I'd seen were quite murky, especially the serpentine Amazonian rivers. But this waterfall and pool were very clear. Don Luis approached the site with gentleness and reverence. As soon as he got close to it, the rain stopped. He started to chant in a language we did not understand, which must have been an old dialect. Even the boy was listening attentively. Don Luis made offerings to the spirits of the place again and went to a large flat stone that was close to the pool. He took out a bundle from his bag and placed it carefully on the stone. He continued to chant as he laid out the contents of the bundle on a cloth, making a carefully orchestrated mandala-like form with the objects. The boy had been sent to gather fresh flowers and plants, and they were placed beautifully within the mandala. Joni and I watched this unfold in complete silence and fascination.

Don Luis came up to me and gently took my necklace off. It was a small chain with a cross that my grandmother had given me to celebrate my first communion. The chain had broken a few times and been replaced, but the cross was the same one she had given me as a child. I had been having problems with my mother, who had adopted the catholic church as her spiritual foundation, and I was confused about which tradition I belonged to. "Honor them both," grandmother had told me when she gave me her gift. "They are both part of you now. Always honor the tradition in which you were born. In your case, you have two. You are a lucky girl," she said with her warm smile. "Your heart will find a way to embrace them, Carmen," she told me respectfully. "It is important to learn from the Old Ways and the New Ways. Together they will make your life whole." She died soon after, and this was the last gift she had given me. I had totally forgotten about this conversation with grandmother, and I wore the cross now more as habit, not for any particular significance. As soon as don Luis touched it, I remembered everything. He held the necklace gently in his hands, and offered it up to the sky in his open palms. Then he carefully placed it at the centre of the mandala on the flat stone.

Don Luis signalled Joni and me to come closer. The boy stood near him in a semi-trance state. He was waiting to do as his maestro asked, and for an instant I saw great wisdom in the boy, as if a different spirit came over him. He stood completely still and attentive. There was a majestic air about him that did not match his young age. Joni grabbed my hand as we approached the natural altar. An array of emotions washed over me. What in the world was happening? For a moment doubt crept in - maybe going into the jungle with a shaman wasn't such a great idea. What if I was going to be a sacrifice? Did they do that in these parts? My imagination went wild until Joni squeezed my hand and brought me to my senses. When we got close to the stone, we naturally kneeled beside it. Don Luis started to blow tobacco smoke over us. He continued to recite some prayers, and we remained silent.

When he was done with his opening ritual, he spoke to Joni in Spanish in a clear and slow voice. Joni translated, "This ritual is for you, Carmen. I am to be your translator and midwife. " She looked towards don Luis for more, and she continued, "You have passed through the Valley of Death. You had a choice between life and death, and you have chosen to live. It is customary to have a baptism for the one who goes through such a journey. It is believed that without this ritual, a person has never fully gone through the birth canal into her new life. What you know of your old self must be left behind in order to let your soul claim its new life." Joni looked at me with big eyes. The shaman asked if I understood. I wasn't quite sure what to respond or what that meant. He continued and Joni translated:

"You have some attachments still to your old life. A part of you remains there. We can break those ties if you wish. Then you will remember much of what happened to you in the in-between places and your life's purpose. Your soul has chosen to live. Now it is you, Carmen, that must choose life. This is what the pool is for. You shall bathe in this pool, and it will cleanse you. It will renew you. She is your mother's womb, the birth place of your soul."

As he spoke these words, memories started to flood back. My expression must have been out of the ordinary because Joni immediately asked if I was alright. I nodded to reassure her. Don Luis took a penetrating look at me, looking deep within me with laser vision. He nodded as well and said, "She remembers." It was Joni now that looked confused, yet intrigued. I started to tell Joni what I remembered, but don Luis stopped me. "Not now. Save it for later. Now, you must go in the water."

He took Joni aside and gave her some instructions. At first she looked as though she was arguing with him. Then she relaxed and listened attentively. I could tell she was taking whatever he was telling her seriously. After a long while and communication back and forth, she came close to me. I looked at her expectantly.

"I am to stay here with you. The sun will set soon, and we are to remain on the rock by the pool until such a time when you are ready to go in the sacred water. You will know when the time is right, he said. We are to stay here overnight and return to the village when the sun comes up." She searched her memory to make sure she hadn't forgotten anything.

"Well that doesn't sound too bad," I said.

Joni looked at me apprehensively, "They will be heading back there soon. We will be alone here."

"You have got to be kidding me!" Terror struck me like a bolt of lightning. "And you agreed to this? Are you insane? We are in the middle of nowhere! There are creepy crawlies around, and you and I barely know how to work a Swiss army knife. Ok well, one of us doesn't." All the calm and confidence of the last few days since I had awoken from the coma left me as soon as I heard that. Joni shrugged her shoulders but didn't respond more than that. I looked for don Luis and the boy, but by the time I located them, they had already packed up their things and were making their way back up the ravine. I yelled after them, calling for their attention, but they both ignored me and continued on their way.

I really started to panic. What in the world? Is this a betrayal? Even Joni went along with this. How could she? I was beside myself.

"Calm down, Carm. It's gonna be alright," Joni tried to reassure me. I wasn't convinced she totally believed that.

If I weren't so tired and hungry, I would have grappled her on the flat rock right there and then. All I could think to do was to calm my breathing, or else I was sure I would hyperventilate. Joni was usually comforting, but now she seemed aloof. I had never felt so alone and vulnerable in my life.

I started to be sick. I kept throwing up and then dry heaving. Joni kept quiet and handed me water to stay hydrated. I cried, and cried, and threw up. It felt like an intense purge. I felt so betrayed, I had no words to explain. And I was so angry, I yelled at the top of my lungs. I admit I was glad we were in the middle of nowhere. My turmoil could likely be heard for miles. Joni kept calm beside me, caring for me, not saying a word but not missing a single beat. This purging continued throughout the night. I didn't know what had taken over me. Maybe don Luis had put something in the water. I could not think straight. My soul was on fire, and my body was purging some elusive poisons. A dog came by and stayed close to us. He was an odd fellow, but somehow he felt familiar. Joni recognized him and greeted him kindly. It was as if he was protecting us.

As the night progressed, I started to feel better. I felt lighter, more fluid, more authentic, and more awake. Memories started to come back: being with grandmother, Angie, Mother Earth, and Amaru…

"Amaru!" I cried out loud, startling Joni. I lay my body down with my belly directly touching the stone. "Come, Amaru. I need you." I remembered how the great serpent spirit had taught me to summon her. I reached out to her in my mind like calling a cosmic 911.

As fast as I had made that wish, I heard the rustling of leaves and a large boa came out to meet us. I thought Joni would faint. Now it was I who was comforting her, "This is Amaru. She won't hurt us." How I knew this I was not sure, but I knew she had eaten not long ago and had come in peace. As the great snake circled the rock we were on, I started to remember more details of my journey until it became crystal clear. And then I realized that this was what I had been fighting for; it was a battle of remembrance. I wanted to remember. I wanted to live. I wanted to live my life consciously and with the gifts that had been given to me. As soon as I felt this in my blood, in my bones, in my heart, mind and soul, I stripped naked and jumped into the clear pool. It was surprisingly cool and refreshing, yet very dark. I stayed submerged as long as I could and then came up for air like a dolphin. It was the most ecstatic moment of my life.

I laughed and laughed. I swam in that pool with so much joy, as if I was taking my first breaths of life. Joni sat on the stone astonished, watching me in wonder. She was no longer concerned with the boa, who was merely a few feet away. Perhaps she had forgotten about it. I asked her to join me. At first she hesitated, unsure what she was meant to be doing. But after a bit of reflection, she took off her clothes and came to swim with me. We played in the water like two children, revelling in the freedom and beauty of the moment. We knew we were experiencing something unique, something sacred. And we didn't have to say anything to one another. We simply knew.

The first ray of light was appearing on the horizon when we got out of the water. We put our clothes back on and rested there for a while. Dog was still nearby. Boa had gone on her way. It was Joni who spoke first.

"How do you feel?"

I smiled. I still could not speak. I was still relishing in this exquisite experience. I remembered everything that had happened after the snake bite, my travel to the life-between-life place, and especially my time with Mother Earth. And I had left my old self behind. I was ready to move on. Joni sensed this, so we picked up our belongings and started to leave. Just as we got off the stone, I noticed the boa had shed her skin. The old one was lying on the ground next to the stone. I took it as an auspicious sign, a confirmation of what occurred to me in that pool and a blessing from Amaru.

Just as we were leaving, I remembered to thank the spirits of this precious place. Both Joni and I kneeled and prayed, knowing we had experienced something extraordinary. We still could not put the experience into words. Feeling full and nourished, we got up to go.

"So, now we need to find our way back to the village. It's only a full day's walk in that direction," Joni waved pretty much in all directions.

"No problem," she said. "We can do this." For once, I agreed with her. I knew it sounded crazy and the old Carmen would have been paralyzed with fear and anger.

"Alright. Let's find our way back. One step at a time. I seem to recall coming down this way. Let's see where it leads," I suggested.

Joni smiled, "Yes, ma'am! Lead the way."

We made it up to the ledge and looked upon the waterfall for the last time. And soon after we came upon the spot that don Luis had had his first ritual to announce our arrival to the spirits of the place. They had left us some water bottles and a pouch of familiar leaves to chew on. We gratefully put the water bottles in our bags and started to chew on the leaves. We left some as offering to the spirits.

"What now? Do you remember where to go?" I asked Joni.

"Not sure, Carm. It looks like there is a path over here," she pointed. And just as she was pointing, Dog came out from the forest.

"Hello, Dog!" I exclaimed, finally recognizing my faithful companion. He wagged his tail.

"He was continually nearby when you where in a coma," Joni mentioned. "The villagers were quite surprised as this creature is usually very shy and rarely interacts with them. They thought you may have a certain medicine that attracted him."

"I remember him," and I proceeded to tell Joni about him.

"Do you think he knows the way home?" Joni asked.

I looked at Dog and communicated with him like I did when I was in spirit form. "He says he knows the way and will lead us there."

It rained on and off all day. The way back was enjoyable. We saw so many creatures there were too many to count. They were so beautiful. The vegetation was so rich we could have spent months classifying all the fauna that lived in a square mile. My favourite were the birds. Joni would notice almost every single plant she came across and give them fictitious names. She said she had learned that trick from an old herbalist. He had told her that giving a name to an unknown plant personified and developed a relationship with it until one could learn their common and scientific names. She jotted down notes here and there. So on our way back the trail was filled with "Sunshines", and "Bobs", and "Shirleys", and "Small Noble Ones". The names she would give these plants were varied and rather hilarious. She took this very seriously and was like a child in wonderland.

Dog faithfully led the way like an experienced tour guide. He sensed when we tired and let us rest and was patient as we took the time to look at the birds or inspect a new insect.

Once, he stopped dead on the trail, with his hair standing up, growling. Before him was a bright fuzzy spider. At first I was taken aback by Dog's reaction, expecting to find a much larger danger, but I had certainly learned not to take any creature in the Amazon for granted. Joni and I stopped and watched. Dog would not let us near the spider. He growled and barked and waited until the spider went scurrying into the forest. After it had gone, Dog went closer and sniffed the ground. Seemingly satisfied, he sat and waited for us to come closer.

"Looks like we are good to go," Joni remarked.

"What do you think that was?" I wondered as we continued walking.

"It looked like a Brazilian Wandering spider, but I am really not sure," Joni answered. "I saw a picture of it in my Lonely Planet guide book. Apparently they are quite dangerous. Dog must know these things instinctively. How clever!"

We both felt grateful and much safer in Dog's company. As we continued walking, Joni and I chatted like school girls catching up on our individual experiences since the accident. I listened in awe as Joni recounted her side of the story. As she spoke, I felt a reverence and deep respect for this woman I had barely known before we set out on this adventure. And here we were talking like old soul sisters. Her experiences were rich, deep and fascinating. Although on the exterior she had not gone through such a dramatic experience as I had, her inner journey was just as transformative. She confessed how stifled she had felt teaching nursing in an establishment. All those years she had taken solace that she was serving her life's purpose by helping others so they in turn could help others. But deep down, she always felt she had a much deeper relationship with healing. And she proceeded to tell me of a near death experience she had had when she was twelve years old. I listened in total amazement. I had no idea! We had never discussed any of this before.

"I haven't told many people," Joni shared. "It was so personal, and frankly I barely remembered it much until I did the Ayahuasca ceremony the other day. Then everything started to flood in like this heavy rain."

It had started to rain heavily again. She continued telling her story.

"I had serious asthma as a child. One spring day, I was out on a school field trip and the pollen count must have been abnormally high because I had a full-blown asthma attack. I was rushed to the hospital, but my lungs gave out. The medics tried to revive me but couldn't. I saw all this happening, hovering over them in the ambulance as they were doing their work. I saw them working on me and talking as if I had died. I did not know what was going on. Out of nowhere I saw a great light and was drawn to it. I went to an in-between place where three beings of light awaited me. They spoke to me gently and told me they were here to help. They said my time on Earth wasn't over yet and that one day I will become a true healer. But not yet. One of the beings put their hands on my chest and took out some dark stuff. Then another blew a clear pulsing light into my lungs. They told me a few things, and then the next thing I knew I was in the emergency room staring at some really stunned medical staff. They had already pronounced me dead and to see me breathe had given them the shock of their lives. Many said it was a miracle. I just wanted to go home. My mother came to get me a while later. It took her that long to reach me. A teacher had stayed with me. I never spoke of this again or the fact that I have never had another asthma attack to this day."

She stopped, and we remained silent for a while. This woman was so full of surprises. There was sadness in her tone, a longing I could not identify. I patiently waited for her to continue.

"When I met the shaman, Carm, I knew I belonged here. I knew I was meant to learn from him. And that I could not deny the potential of healing within me. I knew I simply could not return to academia. That part of my life is over for me now."

She smiled wholeheartedly. Then she stopped walking and looked straight at me, "Carm, thank you. I know it has been a tough road for you. Thank you for your journey because what you have gone through has helped me awaken to who I am." She hugged me tenderly.

I was touched by her gesture. Who was she kidding? I was here because of her. Her courage, integrity and keen ability to make wise choices were what had kept me alive.

"Joni, it is you I should thank. Without you I would not be here. Truly."

We both understood in that moment that our lives were linked, that our souls had contracts to enliven and awaken one another. The two of us, led by a strange dog in the middle of the rainforest, were linked in a way that defied the normal concepts of time, space and relationship. We could not deny this loving connection between us. These were no ordinary coincidences and events. Dog looked at us and yelped as if he understood what we were thinking and experiencing.

"Alright, the three of us are linked," I told him tenderly. Dog was satisfied and continued to lead the way.

CHAPTER TWENTY-ONE

The three of us continued to walk in the jungle at a rhythmical pace. It was getting near the end of the day, and for the first time I started to wonder if we were doing the right thing trusting a dog to lead us back to the village.

"Joni? Do you think we are on the right track?" She looked at me puzzled.

"Your guess is as good as mine. But Dog here seems to be a good tracker, and I did recognize some plants and flowers I had seen before. The way feels oddly familiar to me, but I could be wrong," she shrugged and continued to walk.

"Do you realize these leaves are the only thing we've eaten in a long time?" My stomach grumbled loudly.

"I'd love some of that plantain dish they have in the village," Joni responded dreamily.

"How about some fruit?" I said, looking up a nearby tree.

Joni stopped dead in her tracks. "Carm! You are my star! I've seen these in the village, and they are delicious. Let's get some!"

The following moments were comical. Two determined and very hungry gringo girls trying to get fruit from a tall tree. We tried many things to get the fruit until we eventually found a large and long-enough stick to knock them down. We had a feast. It was the most satisfying and delicious meal I could remember. We were delighted. The fruit revitalized us instantly.

After our snack, we continued walking. The sun was already starting to fade on the western horizon. Then Joni whispered:

"Carm, do you smell that?"

The smell was unmistakable because it reminded me of my grandmother. It was woodsmoke!

We ran. Dog followed us. The closer we got to the smell, the more certain we were we had found our destination. We ran straight into the beloved village and went towards the central square. It looked like everyone was waiting for us. Chickens were roasting on an open fire, and the people were preparing food for what seemed like a feast. We had made it back!

At the sound of cheering, many other villagers came over to greet us. It was a welcoming committee like no other. The children were swarming all around us. Joni already had a small girl in her arms and two other children wrapped around her legs, and others begged me to do the same. Don Luis was waiting for us near the fire. He smiled and looked genuinely pleased to see us. Joni sat near the fire and got busy telling the story of our adventure to keenly listening ears. She was truly in her element. The shaman's apprentice was particularly fond of her and treated her like an older sister.

After the commotion eased up a little, I looked for Dog. He had stayed close to the edge of the forest, preferring not to bring attention to himself. I saw his glowing eyes and sent him waves of gratitude. He was lying down under some thick brush. I asked Joni to ask one of the children for a bowl of fresh water. I offered it to Dog, and he lapped it up with earnest appreciation.

"You are a wonderful companion. We could not have done this without you. Wait, we'll bring you something to eat soon." He drank some more and as if he understood, he lay there comfortably and fell asleep.

I walked back slowly towards the crowd. I was grateful for being alone in that moment, absorbing the precious scene before me. This place felt like home. These people, who had graciously taken us in, treated us like their own, like family. And it looked like we were about to have one heck of a family feast. The scent of roasting chicken reached my nose, and instantly my stomach growled. I was famished.

An abundant array of food was laid before us, and everyone dug in joyously. The women passed around dishes. It was like a game for the children, and they took turns putting some food on our plates. Joni and I were well fed that night. It didn't take much to fill me, as my stomach had become accustomed to small meals. Once everyone had eaten, I noticed there was quite a lot of food left over. I immediately thought of Dog, but wasn't sure if it was culturally accepted to feed a "wild" animal with the villagers' food. I went to don Luis and tried to explain myself using a few Spanish words I had picked up along the way. I did my best to communicate my intent. After using random words and a lot of sign language, it seemed like he understood. He went to the roasted meat and took a generous portion, which he placed lovingly on my plate. He lowered his eyes in prayer before he handed it to me, then nodded.

I took the plate to where I had seen Dog last. He was still there lying by the bush, and as soon as he saw me coming, he jolted up and sat. His jaw smacked in expectation. He must have caught the scent of his dinner. I laid the plate before him, but he did not move. He looked at me as if asking for permission to eat his meal. I nudged the plate closer to him.

"Eat, my friend. You have earned it. Eat to your heart's content." It didn't take more encouragement than that. I waited until he was done eating his meal. To my surprise, he came, and lay down beside me and let me pet him. We both fell asleep, content and happy.

The sound of drumming woke me up. For a moment I thought I was in the centre of the earth with Amaru and Mother Earth again. I floated in between two worlds lulled by the sound of the beat. Dog licked my arm, and this brought me back to the forest. I stood up, refreshed. Dog went on his way, and I was drawn to the fire like an insect to an intense light in the darkness. I followed it. I must have slept for a longer time than I thought because the little ones were now in bed. All that were left around the fire were the adults, and I noticed Felipe was sitting beside Joni. They both waved me over. It was nice to see a familiar face although I had not spoken with him very much. Joni had told me he had played an important role in my recovery by going back and forth and getting supplies. I had not seen him since we were at the Lodge. As I approached, he got up and greeted me with a warm embrace.

"Carmen! It is good to see you!" It was nice to hear another person speak English besides Joni. "You have become a legend around here already. Although tourists now take extra precautions before they head out into the forest," he laughed. "That's okay. Every once in a while, Mother Amazon reminds us not to take her for granted and have respect. That's not a bad thing." He had a beautiful disposition. I was surprised I hadn't noticed it before. He took my arm and put it in his, and together we sat by the fire. I was surprised to feel my heart flutter and my face flush.

The atmosphere around the fire was jovial, and the chicha flowed generously. I was handed a cup and took a sip. The alcohol hit me instantly. It was refreshing and relaxing. Felipe told me the chicha made in the village was legendary for its flavour and potency. It didn't take me many sips to agree. If my face was flushed before, at least I could blame it on the drink now. Felipe sat beside me all night, and it was nice to have a conversation. Joni was speaking fluently in Spanish now, and she was listening to the stories shared in the village for generations. Most of the stories told so far were comical ones, ranging from current characters in the village to some ancestral ones.

Things like what happens if you drink too much chicha and listen to a talking alligator (which made everybody laugh very hard) to the woman who tried over and over again to teach her husband how to weave ancestral designs, but all he managed to make were phallic symbols. (Which made the women laugh even harder, but the men didn't laugh as hard.) Within the stories were always life lessons. It was a way of transferring knowledge in a symbolic way. People loved them.

Then the atmosphere got calmer and quieter. Don Luis reached for his drum, and as if by an invisible cue everyone became silent. Felipe took my hand in his, "Listen! You are in for a treat."

Don Luis started to drum slowly and deliberately. Each beat resonated in my bones, making my body buzz and come alive. The sound and beat reminded me of Amaru, and I felt compelled to listen even more deeply. I could see he was communing with All that Is, with the fire, the land, the people assembled there in a circle around the fire. The stars became brighter, and the jungle more quiet and still. I could see the Web of Life linking us together. I could sense the Great Darkness holding all life together. I was reminded of my time with Mother Earth, and I felt grateful and peaceful. Everyone listened. Everyone was quiet. Even the forest creatures and the elements listened.

Don Luis started to speak, and Felipe translated, whispering in my ear.

"Listen carefully, my people. This is a transmission that has been given to me by my grandfather and his grandfathers before him. This knowledge goes all the way back to the seed origin of our people. I am the keeper of this knowledge, and you are charged to embody it and keep it alive within you. Open your hearts and minds and be the crucible of this teaching." The silence became deeper still. He continued:

"Long ago the Original People occupied this Earth in peace and harmony. They knew the laws of nature and abided by them. Each member of the community lived to share their wisdom and experiences with the young ones. They were also taught by Nature Herself because there was still a good relationship with the sacred Mother back then.

Mother Earth would tell her children many stories. They would gather in a way similar to how we are doing now. You see, story telling is a long-standing art of transmission of truth that belongs to the oral wisdom teachings of our people. All Original People of the planet have and know this art. Although our stories differ in detail and environment, their soul remains the same. Throughout time, generations, cycles, and peoples, the soul of life has nourished itself with these living stories. This is one such story." He paused, drank a bit of chicha, and smoked his pipe.

"There has always been a "shaman", a walker between worlds, the one who serves his community by devoting him/herself to being a hollow bone for the communication among all of life. In the early days, no such person was necessary. Once the fire was lit, a Being would show up as the teacher. Many times it was the Mother herself, and at a few precious occasions the great Wiracocha himself would come and teach. Every being in creation had something to tell. At times, it was a passing turtle, and at others it was a member of the tribe. But the great teachings were often transmitted by the Shining Ones, our brothers and sisters that live amongst the stars." And at this, he blew some of his tobacco smoke high above towards the heavens.

"Our education, our learning, came from many places. The Web of Life was still intact back then. It was not only healthy and intact on the Earth, but also the interplanetary and intergalactic webs reached deep within the earth. Through time, and especially in the last few thousand years, these webs have grown apart. It is due to an important phase in human evolution prophesied by not only our people and ancestors, but also by all those whose roots are from the original people.

In our tradition, in the Quechua language we call eras or worlds "pachas". This is the era of pachakuti, loosely translated as time of great change or the Great Turning."

I gasped when I heard this. I remembered Mother Earth mentioning this in my journey. I was enthralled by don Luis' words. They seemed to have a life of their own, and my imagination was transported in a sensory experience with each word he spoke. It was as if I were in the story with him. Felipe was doing such a good job translating, I even forgot he was translating for me. I took a quick glance at the others around the fire, and it was clear I was not the only one absorbed in the story.

"It is said these are times of great upheaval. Our ancestors could see this coming, and there are only a few that know the reason why these upheavals are occurring. There are certain mysteries that are kept out of our perceptions and knowledge for the sake of our souls' journeys." He paused once more to smoke from his pipe and have a drink of chicha, creating a dramatic pause in the story. We all waited for more.

"But there are some who have made the journey between the veils, and this is what they say: The winds of change are upon us. They blow from the North West, from deep within the realm of the Great Wiracocha and beyond, beyond into the Living Universe, into the Great Mind of the Creator/Creatrix. There used to be many portals that led us to these places, but many have now been closed in preparation for these changes. The Earth is now at a tipping point, and many are watching from beyond the Stars. Many are gathering in what is commonly known as the Inter-Galactic council. In this council there are some who have participated in the creation of this and other worlds. These times are important for the evolution of the soul of humanity and also for the Universal Soul. As each individual soul is connected to the whole, this change is also occurring in the individual lives of the people of Earth. Even in this village, we are feeling this great change occurring. The forest tells us of it, and so do the winds. And so does our beloved Pachamama, Mother Earth.

In her we must trust. For in her lies the truth of the tides of change. Many are watching from high above. Many have gathered to take notes. Those of us alive today are agents of this change, and we are charged with embodying the ancient wisdoms of the Original People and breathing them into the world. It is said that no-one knows what course humanity will take. The future is written in the past. Great Mystery has her hands in the matter. In Her we must trust.

Some say there is no hope for humanity. Some say we have swung the pendulum too far from the centre. Some say the destruction of the world was always meant to happen. Some say that human destiny is in the hands of humanity, that through cause and effect humanity has created its own demise. Some say the Divine Spirit can intervene. Some say It will not.

Truth is, very few know the truth of mankind's destiny. It is a well guarded secret. And those who know will not tell; they will only witness. Whether humanity perishes by its own hands or thrives, there is no judgement. In one way or another we will make our way home towards the light."

As he said this, he waved his hand towards the fire, and as he did so, the fire transformed into a spiralling light reaching far into the sky. Everyone watched.

"Our ancestors have predicted this time. It was going to happen no matter what we had or could have done. The future is past, and the past is future. If you look into the fire you will see."

And at that, don Luis placed a dried powder in the fire that made it burst into yellow flames. It smelled of sulphur. It was as if history was being lived backward and forward at the same time. Each of us, sitting at the fire, were taken back in time and through time. Our souls were the common point. Then time and space collapsed unto each other. There was no time, no space, only a voice coming from the fire, which continued:

"Why does it matter what the fate of humanity is? Do not pretend to know the future. Many say it is already written. The dreamers know otherwise. The future belongs to the Dreamers of Life. What kind of dreamer are you?"

Then within the fire images of the Earth appeared. I don't think I was the only one seeing this because everyone else was looking at the fire in astonished amazement, and Felipe was holding my hand so tightly I thought the circulation would stop.

The images of Earth took many shapes. There were many possible futures. We saw the Earth destroy herself. We saw humanity get to a point of extinction. We also saw a great shift in consciousness, where many human beings would die, and some would be reborn in other places. We saw a slow process where humanity learned once more to live in harmony with itself and all of life. We also saw the possibility of more wars, big destructive wars. The possibilities were endless.

Then out of the fire came a familiar consciousness. It was Mother Earth in her glory. She shone like a star, our beloved planet in the vastness of space. She held her children tight, sending rays of protective love. Her call to her maker was so strong that help was on the way. But best of all, the light shone within the people of Earth, within those who had chosen to protect her and all her relations. I saw myself, I saw Joni, I saw our little group gathered here answering the calling of the

Earth, the calling to live a good life, to courageously embrace the arduous journey of growing a soul.

Then the images disappeared, and I was back by the fire with chicha in my hand. I put my cup down. Don Luis continued.

"You have all seen what you needed to see in the fire." How did he do this I wondered? Felipe and I looked at one another, and I was sure he was as enchanted as I was.

"Remember what you have seen. Remember what Mother Earth and our star relatives wanted to share with you tonight. For this is the way it is done. Each of you carries a spark of the Truth of Life and has a responsibility to the evolution of humankind. It is up to you to choose it, to volunteer for it. And you will not be judged either way. Choose the path that belongs to you."

As he spoke, great lights shone behind him. One could make out some shapes, and soon three beings of light appeared. The place felt small for a moment, very small. Their presence was majestic. I knew in that instant that they were our star relatives, who had gone through much of the same evolutionary growth pains as us, and they were here as big brothers and sisters to help us through this adolescent evolutionary experience, just as they had experienced. They were here to guide us, teach us, and witness an important transition moment in our history.

"We are not alone, my children," don Luis resumed in a fatherly tone.

"We have never been alone. Remember your Origin. Remember the Brotherhood. Remember your role in this time of Pachakuti. What matters is how you play the game of life. What matters is how you live and what you chose to do with your life. Are you helping in the evolution of humanity towards it divine expression or are you hindering it. Which team are you on?

When you decide, play the game of life the best you can. Remember this is a time of duality, so you must pick a side. Or perhaps you want to stay and witness? There will be time for that."

He looked straight at me when he said that. I understood what he meant because of my journey to the life-between-life world.

"For now, realize you are merely a passer-by on this Beautiful Earth. What kind of guest are you? Show the beauty of your soul. The Earth is there to remind you of this. She helps you remember the beauty of who you are."

And at that, the beings of light said their farewell and dissolved like mist into the starlit evening sky.

The sounds of the forest came back into focus, and I heard the drum beat once more. Had someone been drumming all this time? I had been so absorbed in the story that I had not noticed. Slowly everything came back to normal. The drumming stopped, and don Luis put more herbs in his pipe. And he asked for more chicha.

Felipe finally stopped squeezing my hand. I felt an odd silence, and I also realized that he had been translating for me all along. A woman came along and refreshed our cups, and we drank in silence. I looked for Joni and saw her merely sitting in silence. A child had fallen asleep in her lap. We looked at one another and did not need to say a thing; we both knew this had been an extraordinary experience.

"Hey, Felipe! What else is in this chicha? " I asked playfully. We both laughed. "I told you we were in for a treat," he smiled.

CHAPTER TWENTY-TWO

The following day I woke up refreshed and filled with wonder and simplicity. My body was strong again, and I hadn't felt that good in years. I was now sharing a hut with Joni because I no longer needed to be in the healing lodge. Joni must have gotten up at the crack of dawn and gone to gather some plant medicines with the boy. She really didn't skip a beat.

It was a beautiful, warm sunny day. I got out of the hut and took a deep breath. I wanted to take in each precious moment. I was so grateful for being where I was. The moment I stepped out of the hut, some children were around me. Felipe was just coming out of the other guest house to my right. He must have stayed the night. I didn't remember much about last night after the story had finished. I must have fallen asleep exhausted. Felipe mirrored my thoughts:

"Good morning, Butterfly! Did you rest well?"

"Hmm, yes, thank you," I stuttered.

"You were tired last night. Fell asleep by the fire. I took you home," he laughed unabashed.

I blushed. That was embarrassing. I barely knew this guy. Did I get drunk and made a fool of myself? It wasn't my thing, but you never know.

"You were asleep very soon after the story ended," he clarified, seeing my discomfort. "Your previous journey must have taken a lot out of you," he winked.

Now a few of the boys were around him, wanting to play a form of football. He pretended not to be strong or big enough to play with them, which made the children more determined to get him out on the field. He shrugged and surrendered. "See you later," he smiled.

"See you later," I stuttered again behind a blushing face.

What was wrong with me? Why was I reacting this way to this man? It was out of character for me. So I brushed it off as some kind of Amazonian by-product or something.

Felipe was right. My journey, as he called it, certainly had taken a lot out of me. Only yesterday, Joni and I were walking back from the waterfall. So much had happened in the last few days and weeks, I wasn't sure what to make of it all yet. I thought of Dog and went to see if I could find him. For some reason I really missed his company. I was sad to see he was not in the area where I had seen him last. I went down to the river, sat on the dock, and watched the water flow by. I needed more time by myself, time to contemplate for the first time in my life. It was good to slow down. If I had continued at the pace I had been living, I would have missed out on essential living. I was not living a good life. These few weeks in the Amazon had changed all that, and I was grateful.

A little hand pulled my shirt. She indicated it was time for breakfast. A different family had "adopted" Joni and me each day to feed us, and today it was her turn. The girl was very proud, and her smile beamed brighter than the sun.

We had a breakfast of roasted plantain, fresh fruit and some left-over chicken from last night's feast. I was not sure what this family used for seasonings, but it was delicious. I ate rabidly and hoped I wasn't being impolite. To the contrary, they were pleased to see me eat so much and kept putting more food on my plate. The girl nodded to the bushes nearby where Dog was poking his head out of some greenery. That was bold for him, I thought, especially in daylight. The mother instinctively put chicken bits on a plate and handed it to me. I was delighted to bring Dog some breakfast.

The day went by slowly. I immersed myself in village life doing chores, learning more Spanish, and playing with the children. Felipe returned to the Lodge but said he would be back soon. In a way I was relieved that he was leaving the village. I found his presence distracting. Joni teased me about it. I told her to go learn about new plants.

Days passed. It was not long before I found my full strength restored and then some. The rest of the tour group had already flown back to their respective homes. It had been forty days since we arrived in Peru. It felt like a lifetime. So much had happened. Joni and I sat by the dock, looking onto the mighty river. The sun was setting, and it was particularly beautiful that night. The wind blew softly, and the air was thick with life.

"We had our own tour of Peru," Joni said breaking the silence. "It was unexpected, but no tour could have given us this rich experience."

"Tell me about it. I was just following you along, Joni. I only wanted to get away from home, from my life, from everything. I never thought I would find meaning here. I thought you were a little nuts to be seeking spiritual awakenings with a tour group. Now that I am here, I understand. This place is vibrant with wisdom, meaning, and truth. Its soul is still alive. Although much of the Peruvian people have forgotten their own traditions and culture, a few pockets of ancient wisdom still remain. And we are in one of them."

There were a few modern amenities in the village, clues that the people were living in the 21st century, but their traditions remained. Their spirit remained. The connection with the ancestors remained. And don Luis, the shaman was the living force behind helping his people remember who they are.

At that moment sitting in the sunset, we knew that we had entered in a bubble of timelessness. But soon our world would come back to us. We both sensed this but did not want to speak of it until it was inevitable. I broke the ice.

"I know we don't want to talk of this, Joni, but I think it is time that we return to Canada soon," I said quietly.

"I know, Carm. I've been thinking about that too."

"So where to from here?" I asked, almost afraid to hear her answer.

"I don't want this to end," Joni replied pensively, "but I know the end of this cycle is fast approaching. It is time to go home soon, but I am not going back to teaching."

I was shocked by her response. She sounded so certain. She saw my look and explained.

"For years I was looking for a way out of my life, and I didn't know it. Don't get me wrong, I appreciate every part of the academic world that I've experienced. Through the years I've helped save the lives of many people and have learned so much about medicine through teaching. But that cycle is over for me. Now it is time to develop the healing abilities that have been lying dormant within me. They have been awakened now, and it is time to change directions." She waited until I digested what she'd said.

"Don Luis has offered to help me learn about healing. He says he can teach me the traditional ways. And I want to. It is time. My medical background is also helpful here. He wants me to help him bridge the two worlds."

"Are you saying you are staying here?"

"No, no," she laughed. "I am coming back with you. I have things to settle and finish up with, but I will be coming back regularly, as a guest and apprentice." She was beaming. I could tell she had spent a lot of time thinking about this, and she was relieved to share it aloud.

"Joni, this is wonderful! I am so happy for you. And it really suits you in a quirky kind of way." I hugged her wholeheartedly. Knowing Joni, she would be genuine and work hard in anything she decided to do. And she deserved to do what made her happy and follow the calling of her soul.

"What about you?" she asked me inquisitively. "Can I come to your wedding?" She smirked.

"What are you talking about? Will you stop teasing me about Felipe?" I was exasperated. She smiled and gave me a sip of her drink.

"I love teasing you. It's so easy. But seriously, have you thought of what you will do when you get home?"

Home. What an odd concept. This village felt more like home than the four walls that held my belongings. As soon as I thought of it, memories of my life came flooding back - my car, my house, my ruined career, my empty life, my estranged mother. Bits and pieces everywhere existing without warmth or cohesion. The only shining piece was Joni, and she was right here with me. I thought of the yoga classes and my token help at the food shelter. What exactly was I going home to? I was facing a life in ruins. I had to go to court to protect what little I had left. It was likely I would not be able to practice in real estate until the trials were over, until I proved my innocence. I had no idea how I was going to manage all this, but something within me knew that I would find a way. That I was meant to go back and make it right, make it whole.

"Carmen?" Joni's voice took me out of my reverie.

"I am going to go back and set things right, Joni. I have been given the gift of life, a chance to honor what I have learned here. I want to give it my best shot," I said this with certitude and confidence, which surprised me.

"I promised Mother Earth, Joni. My life belongs to her now."

Joni gazed at me profoundly. "Yes, you did. And you will fulfill your promise," she smiled knowingly.

Just then, Felipe pulled up in a boat. Joni got up quickly and mumbled about something she had to do. She was already a few feet away when she waved and said hello to him. She winked at me. I looked at her in dismay. Would she ever stop doing that? Felipe came and greeted me warmly. In truth, I was very pleased to see him. He took my hand and wanted to know everything about my day.

At last the time to go was here. We were summoned to see don Luis one last time. It was late in the evening and a fire was lit. Chicha flowed in the glasses of the ones gathered. Joni and I were noticeably nostalgic, not wanting to say goodbye. Felipe was there as well, translating for me, although I could understand a lot more words now.

"You have done well, you two," don Luis told Joni and me. "You have adapted naturally and eloquently to our village and culture, and for this we are grateful." Many people around the fire lifted their glasses in acknowledgment.

"For many years now, we have kept our ways quiet yet not hidden. Gringos have been attracted to the healing powers of Mother Ayahuasca. I have done ceremonies for them a few times yet have chosen to remain in this semi-remote village and teach my people in a traditional way. I did not understand, until now, the healing effects that Ayahuasca has on the mind and heart of the gringo soul. With you two, I see much difference. You have the capacity to heal, cleanse and return in your own way to the heart of Pachamama. It is the spirit of Amaru that guided you here for healing, and it is Her I serve." The people made a toast to these words, as if saying they too served Her.

"Amaru is sacred in our tradition. Her body is the closest to our beloved Pachamama, and her spirit is intimately linked with her as well." He started to drum. "The great Amaru with Mother Ayahuasca have come out of their cave. For years, my ancestors and I have been the guardians of her sacred medicine. It had become so natural for us, that we took it for granted. We did not realize the world may need her medicine. Until recently, this was true. It was our cosmic and earthly charge to care for her, and this was enough to sustain balance for the entire planet. But now Amaru has asked to be set free in the world, into the hearts and minds of the people of Turtle Island and beyond. We are one land, one people." I must make a point to ask Joni or Felipe about Turtle Island, I though. I hadn't heard the name before. The drumming continued.

"Mother Ayahuasca's spirit has now been released into the world. We are still its caretakers, the ones who will honor her wisdom and wishes. You now have two separate experiences with her: One of you has experienced her in the flesh, and the other has experienced the potency of her spirit without even touching her physical medicine." He looked straight at me. In his gaze I remembered the snake bite and the subsequent journey. Was he saying that this experience came from the Ayahuasca spirit herself? He continued:

"Ayahuasca is a messenger for Mother Earth and of our true origins. She teaches the ways of life and harmony. Her medicine is more needed in the world now than it has ever been. She has awoken, uncoiled herself. She is the daughter of the great Cosmic Serpent. She serves Creation. She is a gift to us to help us remember who we are as Children of Earth and Children of the Sun. As above, so below. As below, so above."

I could sense a deep pulsing from within the earth, moving rhythmically with the sound of the drumming. It was familiar to me, comforting. I knew don Luis was calling the spirit of Amaru. My thoughts dissolved in this calling, and my heart opened to receive this great spirit, who had taught me so much and given me new life. It seemed in that moment that the power of Creation was called forth a thousand fold. Everything exuded it, the pulse of the drum, the life force in the forest, the spirits of a all living creatures. In one swirling motion it was as if the creative impulse from the Earth blended with the one from the Cosmos. And in one precious moment these two worlds merged; the creative power within the Earth was one and the same as the one at the origin of all life in the universe. And we were sitting in between these two forces in a circle around the fire. Like two upside down swirling tornadoes. Everyone was quiet.

Then don Luis asked Joni and me to come closer. He asked a couple of strong women to bring a mat and to stand close to us. He said some prayers while his apprentice continued to drum. He blew tobacco smoke over us to bless and purify us. Then he said "Remember." As he said that, my legs buckled from underneath me. The women caught me and gently laid my body down on the mat. One of them placed a soft piece of clothing under my head. Out of the corner of my eye I sensed that Joni was lying down as well and that she too was in a trance.

The surrounding life force took over me. I thought I may have drunk too much chicha, but I had only had a couple of sips. And I knew better now, I knew it was possible to dream extraordinary experiences into ordinary reality. The shaman's presence was conducive to this, and so was the power of this place.

I dreamt myself back to the time I had first arrived in the Amazon and felt an instant connection. All I had learned since then came back crystal clear.

I stood up with the help of the two women. I wanted to address these beautiful people, to share my experiences and what I had learned over the past few weeks. I stood by the fire, finding my voice, wanting to honor the people who had given me so much. I wanted to give them the gift of my remembrance. I stood, and after a few deep breaths, I looked deep into the people's souls. All I could say was, "Thank you!"

CHAPTER TWENTY-THREE

It was time to say goodbye. Joni and I were standing on the dock, with our belongings packed and stacked in a neat pile near the boat. No one wanted to put them in quite yet. We were covered in flowers, individual flowers in our hair, garlands made of all kinds of flowers offered by the children. There was both joy and sadness in the air. Joni let her tears flow freely while I was being more reserved about it. I had never liked goodbyes and would have preferred to take off quietly and unnoticed.

Then a little girl came to me with an offering. She and her brother had carved a small bowl for me, and on it was a depiction of a dog in the forest. She was the girl who had helped me feed Dog the night of the feast. She remembered how precious he was to me and wanted me to have something to remember him by. I couldn't hold back the tears. My heart was so touched. At first she was taken aback, thinking I was upset with her gift. I reassured her it was beautiful and that I loved it very much. She beamed as she nestled herself in my arms. I let my tears flow, and as I did I looked around at this beautiful place and these people who had collectively taken me in and saved my life. How could I ever repay such generosity?

By living a good and authentic life, my inner voice whispered. By honoring what I had learned, by remembering them. They were the guardians of the forest, the keepers of ancient earth wisdom, and by some unforeseen mystery I had become one of them. It was now my duty to carry this truth within me and honor my pact to be of service to the greater world and to our beloved Mother Earth.

We had come to this village for a reason, don Luis repeatedly told us. And it was time to integrate the teachings we had received with the Western world from which we came. We had something to offer one another, and I intended to play an active part in my new role. In that moment, the meaning of my life became clear, and so did its purpose. And it came from a deep love for these people, for nature, and a deep gratitude for being bitten by Amaru, the great transformer.

At the thought of Amaru I knew I had to say goodbye to the her as well. I gently released the girl from my arms and went towards the forest. Don Luis had showed me how to carry a medicine pouch. I took it out of my bag. No one followed me. It always amazed me that the villagers seemed to know when I needed my solitude.

I found a place with an opening by a tree and made offerings to Amaru, thanking her deeply for her blessing, love, and friendship. For a moment, I felt her within me, and we were moving together once more. I knew our spirits had touched. In a wordless way, I thanked her. The dreamy state was soon gone, and in that moment I knew I would be back one day to see her again. For now, the journey was complete.

Walking back to the dock, I noticed the luggage had been loaded on the boat. Felipe was there waiting for us. I saw him clearly in that moment, his goodness, his soul, his connection to the land and the people. Here before me was a simple man, without many possessions and great ambitions, waiting to take us safely to the Lodge. That simple boat was more beautiful and grand than the most impressive cruise ship. I knew then that I had been taught about the true value of life. I was humbled, grateful, and overjoyed to see Felipe again.

After a great deal of tears, hugs and goodbyes, Joni and I finally got into the boat and waved our farewells. Most of the village had gathered there to see us off. Only Felipe and a couple of younger men, who were going to town to get some supplies, were with us in the boat. Once the boat left the shore, we sat in silence for a while, digesting the experience and letting the tears flow as they may. It was a beautiful morning, and the sun was shining brightly, illuminating the beauty of the forest. I was still surprised to see new species of birds. Soon our sorrow left us, and we were enthralled in the moment once more.

"Do you see that monkey?" Joni pointed excitedly to a low hanging branch near the river. "I'll definitely call that one George. Look how curious he is! He is almost falling off the branch." She jotted down a quick description of George in her notebook. She had expanded her notes to animals now. Her little notebook was now filled to the brim, including scraps of papers, plant samples, and some sketches.

The boat ride was beautiful. All this time in the village and I hadn't ventured this far. Except for the walk to the waterfall and close explorations around the village, I hadn't gone very far at all. It was a treat to be on this mighty river and witness so much diversity. The presence of life, of Mother Earth, was so strong. I could sense her pulsing within me and within the environment. Felipe continued to point at different species, and Joni wrote with vigour in her notebook. Felipe laughed, "Joni! You will need a much bigger notebook next time." Her face had mischief all over it.

I shook my head, "Oh, Joni! I love your passionate nature."

Time stood still. I wanted to take in every single moment and make them last as long as possible. I wasn't sure when I was going to come here again, so every moment became pregnant with expectation and gratitude.

After a couple of hours on the river, we finally reached the Lodge. I couldn't believe it had been almost two months since we first came here. Felipe docked the boat masterfully.

"We're here, ladies and gentlemen." I had almost forgotten about the two men that had joined us. They had fallen asleep as soon as they got on the boat. They helped Felipe tie the boat, said a quick farewell, and went on their way. They still had a long walk ahead of them to the nearest town, or if they were lucky, they would hitch a ride with some local folk.

Felipe had generously offered to drive us to Lima. It was a ways away, but he had business to do there on behalf of the Lodge.

"He just wants to spend as much time with you as possible," Joni teased. Whatever the reason, we were glad to be able to see a little more of the country we had come to visit. The drive would take a few days, so we would stay the night at the Lodge and be on our way back down the river in the morning.

Joni and I were given separate rooms. Even coming to this place was a culture shock. It was by no means fancy but tailored to the tourist with amenities and designs that suited a more worldly expectation. I laughed.

"What's up, Carm?" Joni asked.

"I would have found this place basic at most before. Now it is like we are at the Ritz! I wonder what it will be like to get back to society."

Joni nodded her head, "Yep. Welcome back to the real world!"

And if the "real world" was a Lodge in the Amazon, we were in for a bit of a shock.

"I am going to have a bath," Joni exclaimed dreamily. We both ran to our rooms.

A couple of hours later, I heard a knock on my door. For an instant my heart skipped a beat. I had avoided Felipe since we reached the Lodge, and now I wished it were him. I peaked cautiously through the peephole; it was Joni. I let her in.

"That was divine!" she exclaimed while plopping herself on my bed. "Did you try your bed? It is like swimming in a cloud!" I smiled, handing her a glass of fresh juice. She sat up to drink it.

"I know. That bath was delicious. There were flower petals all around it."

"Really? I didn't have flowers in my bathroom," Joni said inquisitively. "Who put them there I wonder?"

"I thought it was part of the Lodge service," I replied innocently.

"Yeah right, Carm. Who organized this for us?"

I looked at her stupefied. I knew, but I couldn't answer. I wasn't good at that kind of stuff. I had a crush on Felipe, but my rational mind could not justify taking it any further. Besides, I had my life to think about now.

"I figured your experiences of nearly dying and hanging out with Mother Earth would have taught you to start trusting your heart, Carm," she smiled, looking straight through me. This time, I let her. I plopped down on the bed beside her.

"Alright. I do like him, Joni, but this is crazy. We are heading home soon. Why even bother?" She looked at me with compassion.

"Because your heart tells you to. Trust it. And let go of the need to figure it all out. Go for it!"

I breathed deeply. Maybe she was right.

She jumped out of bed. "I'm going to go check this place out and see if I can get some news of the outside world from the gringos," she laughed. Just as she was opening the door to leave, Felipe stood there ready to knock.

"Oh hi, Felipe," she said with emphasis on the 'Felipe'. She scooted out of the room like a hummingbird.

Felipe and I both stood there a little shy until my manners took hold of me, "Come in!"

"Thank you," he said. "I don't mean to disturb you."

"It's okay, Joni was just on her way."

"I hope your stay is comfortable."

"Yes, thank you. Very much."

I could tell he felt awkward. He took a deep breath.

"Will you join me for dinner? I prepared something for you."

For once my heart responded first, "I would love to!"

I was eating breakfast on my balcony when Joni came in. I could smell the coffee as soon as she came through the door.

"Is that coffee?" The last coffee I had had was at the hotel in Lima. I had not thought of it until now. It smelled divine.

"I have a cup for you."

I reached out for it.

"Not so quick, my friend! You have to spill the beans first. What happened last night?"

She can be evil at times. Not fair, I thought.

"Fine. Now hand it over."

Joni scuttled towards me, looking very pleased with herself. I had a grin on my face, and it wasn't just because of the coffee.

The drive to Lima was wonderful. It gave us a chance to see so much more of Peru in a way that most tourists never got a chance to experience it. As usual Felipe was an excellent guide and historian, and combined with Joni's natural inquisitive curiosity, they provided enough entertainment and information that all I did was sit back, listen, and enjoy the ride. It was like watching the making of an episode on the History channel live.

We had recovered from the initial culture shock of being out of the village. We reached Lima in good time even though we took some detours along the way to see some notable historic sites. Felipe was well versed in the colonial roots, as well as the more ancient traditions of his people.

We spent a couple of days in Lima, visiting the sights and Felipe's sister. It was nice to spend time with him, and Joni made excuses a few times, so we could have some time alone. I was a little torn about getting so close to him and having to leave the next day. The entire experience felt surreal. I hadn't gotten involved intimately with a man for years because I had been too busy with my career. I had dated but nothing had traction, and I had been okay with that.

It became clear to me that I had been incapable of authentic love. I was too busy building a castle made of sand to notice the emptiness within me. Now the emptiness had been filled with a new meaning of life.

In a strange way, I was ready to leave Peru. Felipe's confidence in me gave me strength in a way that encouraged me to move forward with courage. He was not concerned at all as to "what would happen" to "us". He said that if the stars had ordained it, there was nothing we could do to keep us apart. As long as we were authentic and true to ourselves, life would find a way to bring us together again.

I knew I had a mess to take care of back in Canada. I could not leave it the way it was. I had to face some potential legal trials and figure out how to rebuild my life.

One thing was certain - I made a promise to Mother Earth that I would honor and practice the gifts of knowledge she had given me, and I would do my best to fulfill that promise, whatever it took.

I spent the last night with Felipe, looking at the ocean from our hotel room. The sun was setting on the western horizon, and I was not sad to see it disappear in the bosom of the waters. Everything had cycles. Death was part of the greater cycle of life. I saw the sunset as a sign of hope that new beginnings will be upon me one day. And I was no longer afraid of the dark, of death, of the Great Mystery. I welcomed it. I was part of the Great Web of Life.

Felipe told me stories about his people late into the night. When he asked me for some stories about my people, I was stumped. Did I have something worthy to tell? Then suddenly I started to feel my blood pulse through my veins. Stories that my grandmother had told me as a child came flooding in. There were so many I wasn't sure where to begin. So I started with my favourite, the one about the canoe-maker. Felipe listened attentively until we fell into an exhausted and ecstatic sleep.

The next morning, I could still feel my ancestors' blood flowing through my veins. Unbeknownst to me a miracle had happened; I had found my roots again. I had connected to my ancestral lineage. I smiled at the irony of coming to Peru to re-member and embrace my own ancestry. But something broke through. I had broken free from the chains I had grown into in-stead of roots. I could feel who I was. I no longer had to hide behind my fears and inadequacies.

One does not realize how damaging and dimming it is to the soul to live a life that is not authentically one's own. I had pushed away my grandmother's love because I made the choice I was better off without it, that without her there to give it to me, I was not able to give it to myself. By shutting myself off to what was true and genuine for me, I had let in what was not. And that became my life, my reality, my perception. Instead of love, I chose pain and fear as the foundation for my life, but that was far from being the truth.

Truth was, I was deeply loved. Grandmother's strong and courageous spirit reminded me of that. And it also reminded me that I was connected to the lineage of my father. His love shone through, and somehow the beauty and simplicity of the relationship with Felipe reminded me of that. I was whole, even with the broken pieces. Wholeness never leaves, and the broken pieces can be mended. Separation wants us to believe that wholeness is not possible, but that is merely an illusion.

All of life is interconnected. This means we are never separate from love and wholeness. Within this great experience is the experience of fear, loneliness, pain and separation. These are wonderful foods for the soul's growth and journey. And as Mother Earth had eloquently requested, "Remember Me." The soul wants to be re-membered.

As I mused about what I had learned and embodied in this miraculous journey, I was content. I knew that my life would be a mess upon my return, that the next days, weeks and perhaps months would be challenging and at times perhaps unbearable, but I was ready for that part of my journey. I was not alone. The sun would rise again, and a new life would be born. I had the power and wisdom to re-member myself. I was a child of the Earth and Stars, and all was well in the eternal moment.

I am Carmen Agnes Sirota, and this is my story.

ACKNOWLEDGEMENTS

I t takes a community to birth a project, and I have many people to thank and be grateful for.

First and foremost, there would not be a book without the persistent nudging from my dear friend, Lorraine Doré, to participate in NaNoWriMo (National Novel Writing Month). Her continuous cheerleading, sense of humour, and companionship offered the perfect alchemical formula that transformed me into a fiction writer. Thank you, Lorraine, from the bottom of my heart.

Oscar Miro-Quesada, my beloved maestro and cherished friend, thank you for being a pristine example of what it means to teach love by the way you live. This book is a result of 'growing corn and potatoes' with the wealth of sacred wisdom you have so generously imparted and transmitted over the years. It's the least I can do.

Lord Ganesha, I can't thank you enough for helping me get out of my own way.

To my editor Evelina Proeva. Thank you for investing so much in this project, for believing in the story, and for applying your word-magic to the manuscript.

Thank you, Greg, for not questioning the countless hours I devoted to this labour of love, and for giving me the space to be and create.

To those who took the time to read the rough first drafts of this book, I am most grateful: Steve Fanning, Elle, Stevo, Jennie Cross, Michele Davison, Kendra Goheen, David Spencer, and Eddie Mallon. Thank you. Your enthusiastic feedback and encouragement gave me strength to keep working.

Most of all, I would like to express my gratitude to Mother Earth. Without your strong spirit, which lives in this book, it would have remained in the ethers of my computer files. You are the one that called me to continue, to not give up. I am your midwife, your caretaker, your sacred messenger. Thank you for entrusting me with this work. I hope I have served you well.

ABOUT THE AUTHOR

Yola Dunne is a traveller between worlds, martial artist, lover of life, and universal shaman. Her in-depth studies in creative arts, comparative religion, natural healing, shamanism, and mysticism have ignited her passion for writing and to teach about the wisdom ways of Earth's original people. When not writing, Yola upholds a private healing practice where she helps clients live fulfilling and authentic lives. She also teaches classes inspired by the Pachakuti Mesa Tradition, and hosts earth-honouring ceremonies and rituals. She lives in Chelsea, Québec.

Yola is also the author of the poetry book *Hymns to the Beloved: A Call for Sacred Love*. This is her first novel.

To reach Yola, to join her eList, or for information about her books, events, and recent musings, visit:

WWW.YOLADUNNE.COM

ABOUT
LOVING MOTHER EARTH PRESS

Inspiring earth stewards one word at a time.
Visit us online:

WWW.LOVINGMOTHEREARTH.COM

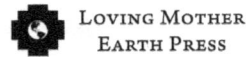

LOVING MOTHER
EARTH PRESS